Boy Trouble
RUMOR CENTRAL
RESHONDA TATE BILLINGSLEY

Dafina KTeen Books
KENSINGTON PUBLISHING CORP.
www.kensingtonbooks.com

DAFINA KTEEN BOOKS are published by

Kensington Publishing Corp.
119 West 40th Street
New York, NY 10018

All Kensington titles, imprints, and distributed lines are available at special quantity discounts for bulk purchases for sales promotion, premiums, fund-raising, and educational or institutional use.

Special book excerpts or customized printings can also be created to fit specific needs. For details, write or phone the office of the Kensington Special Sales Manager: Kensington Publishing Corp., 119 West 40th Street, New York, NY 10018. Attn. Special Sales Department. Phone: 1-800-221-2647.

KTeen logo Reg. U.S. Pat. & TM Off.
Sunburst logo Reg. U.S. Pat. & TM Off.

ISBN-13: 978-0-7582-8959-9
ISBN-10: 0-7582-8959-6
First Kensington Trade Paperback Printing: October 2014

eISBN-13: 978-0-7582-8960-5
eISBN-10: 0-7582-8960-X
First Kensington Electronic Edition: October 2014

10 9 8 7 6 5 4 3 2 1

Printed in the United States of America

Boy Trouble
RUMOR
CENTRAL

Also by ReShonda Tate Billingsley

Rumor Central

You Don't Know Me Like That

Real As It Gets

Truth or Dare

Boy Trouble

Published by Kensington Publishing Corp.

A note from the author . . .

When I started working for the *National Enquirer* tabloid magazine, I had no idea that it would send my imagination into overdrive and help me to one day create a young diva who blows up by dishing celebrity dirt. I left there because, well, I'm not made to dish dirt. But I'm glad for that experience, because it helped shape the stories for the *Rumor Central* series.

I am loving the love you guys have shown for the series so far, and I hope that this fifth book delivers as well. Please tell a friend about the *Rumor Central* series (and tell your teachers, librarians, and everyone else to get it as well!).

In the meantime, let me say a gigantic thanks to my daughters, Mya and Morgan, especially Morgan, who constantly gave me feedback and input! (Mya was always too busy trying to perfect her back handspring.) Thanks to the rest of my family; my friends; my agent, Sara Camilli; my awesome editor, Selena James; my wonderful publicist, Adeola Saul; and all the fab folks at Kensington.

Huge, huge thanks to Gina Johnson, Sheretta Edwards, and Yolanda Gore. I don't know how I would've gotten this book done without your help.

Thank you to Xavier Billingsley, Maya White, and Crystal Turner and much thanks to the terrific readers who pick up my books, tell others, and show me so much love. Big shout-out to all the teen book clubs that choose my books to discuss.

Thank you to the parents, teachers, librarians, and concerned adults who turn teens on to my books. I am so grateful to you.

I can't wrap without sending a huge shout-out to my social media followers. Thanks for the input, for keeping me hip. Your words of encouragement and upliftment keep me motivated, inspired, and encouraged, and show me so much love! A thousand thanks.

Well, that's it for now. Make sure you hit me up and let me know what you think about the series. And if this is your first one, make sure you go back and check it out from the beginning!

Much Love,
ReShonda

Chapter 1

Membership had its privileges. Membership in the "It Clique," that is. And not only was I in the It Clique, I could very well be president. I know some people call the way I am arrogance, but I call it confidence, and I'm one confident chick. But then, again, I am Maya Morgan, the hottest young talk show host in the country. Anyone who had any doubt just needed to check out all the paparazzi clamoring to get a glimpse of my love life at this very moment.

"Maya! Are you and J. Love back together?" one of the photographers shouted in my direction, just as yet another flash went off. I didn't say a word as I followed the security guard back into the VIP section of the club. The photographer was quick, though. He jumped over the rope and started clicking away just as I sat back down.

It didn't take long before security was all over him, dragging him and his camera out.

I kept my signature smile, but I didn't miss how everyone was staring my way. *Oh, yeah, I love my life.* I was the go-to chick in the entertainment industry. And I didn't even need to be in L.A. to claim that title. I was kicking butt and taking names from right here in Miami.

I, the fantabulous Maya Morgan, had made a household name of myself as host of *Rumor Central*, and though many had tried to knock me off my throne, no one had succeeded. That's why I was once again sitting in the VIP with the hottest R & B singer in the country by my side, paparazzi sneaking in, fans going crazy . . . trying to get my picture.

Before I was on-air—first as one of the five members of the *Miami Divas* reality show, then as the host of my own show—I was already at the top of the food chain as one of the most popular teens in Miami. It didn't hurt that my dad was stupid rich—he owned a chain of hotels, which, of course, made me stupid rich. In fact, my popularity was why I'd been approached to get in the reality biz in the first place. Then, *Miami Divas* had tanked (definitely not because of me, though). So, they'd canceled that show, fired the other four Divas, and given me my own show. That had been the smartest thing since the invention of the Internet, because in no time, I had become the go-to chick for all the latest celebrity gossip, dirt, and entertainment news. *Rumor Central* had exceeded everyone's expectations and was now internationally known.

My BFF, Sheridan, had been one of the original *Miami Divas* who had been fired and that had led to a whole lotta drama, but we'd squashed that and were back to kickin' it. I couldn't say the same about the other busters from *Miami Divas*. Shay, Bali, and Evian still had stank attitudes about the way everything had gone down. (They claimed we'd had a pact to stick together and I'd sold them out by taking my own show. Like it was my fault that they were boring.) Besides, they all knew that if the tables were turned, no way would they have turned down the chance to have their own show.

"Hey, what are you thinking about? Hope it's me," whispered J. Love, my ex-boyfriend and date for the night, as he leaned in, snapping me out of my thoughts.

"Of course I'd be thinking about you," I told him. "After

all, you're the most important thing in my life." I flashed a sarcastic smile and he laughed. J. Love was an R & B singer who had to be the hottest thing going right now. He was so fine it was ridiculous. He had smooth chocolate skin, curly hair, and a body that was out of this world. He looked like a much finer version of Trey Songz, with the swag of Chris Brown. Problem was, he knew it.

"You're something else, Maya Morgan."

I just smiled and did a sexy wink. I knew J. was on cloud nine, because he'd been trying and trying to get me to give him a second chance. Long story on why we'd broken up in the first place, but I wasn't trying to give him another chance. However, J. Love hadn't gotten to be a world-famous singer by taking no for an answer. He'd kept after me and I'd finally broken down and agreed to go to this MTV party that we'd both been invited to. My other BFF, Kennedi, was here, too, even though I hadn't seen her butt in the last thirty minutes. That's who I'd been looking for when the paparazzi almost trampled me.

I'd known the paparazzi would eat it up if they saw me and J. Love back together. And I'd been right, too, since the man they had just escorted out was still trying desperately to keep taking pictures of us as they tossed him out.

"You need anything?" J. Love asked as he stood.

"No, I'm good," I replied, leaning back and crossing my long, chocolate legs, which were toned in all the right places. My sequined Vera Wang miniskirt made sure J. could get an eyeful, and he didn't try to hide that he was checking me out.

"Dang, girl. You are so fine." He shook himself out of his trance. "You sure you don't want something to drink?" he asked me again. He'd been trying to pump liquor in me since I'd walked in the door. "This is some good stuff," he added as he held up his cup. I turned up my nose. I didn't need to drink to be cool. I'd said it before and I'd say it again. I didn't need anything to take me off my A game.

I glanced to my left and saw a girl passed out in a booth in the corner—her legs were wide open and someone was taking a picture of her. She would be on MediaTakeOut before she woke up. No, that wouldn't be me. I'd worked too hard to build the Maya Morgan brand, and I wasn't going to blow it over a glass of Patron.

"No, J. Me and my water are just fine," I said, tapping my bottle of Fiji.

"That's why your skin is so beautiful," he said, smiling at me. "All that water you drink."

I smiled. I wanted to say, *Tell me something I don't know*, but I'd been trying to curb my confidence since *Teen People* had recently done an article calling me "arrogant." I couldn't help it if I was all that. But Tamara, my boss at the TV station, had suggested I bring the confidence down a notch.

"Well, well, well, if it isn't Miss Maya 'Snitch' Morgan."

I turned around to the voice that was coming from behind me. I rolled my eyes at the sight of the one person in the industry I simply could not stand, washed-up actress Mynique Foxx. (The child's name was pronounced Monique, but she spelled it with a y trying to be different. It was just stupid if you asked me.)

I couldn't stand her because she couldn't stand me and she made sure to tell anyone who would listen how she really felt about me. Mynique had been on a hit TV show eight years ago, but her star had definitely fallen. Now, she did straight-to-DVD movies. So, I didn't sweat that one-hit wonder and her funky attitude because as the comedian Katt Williams said, If you don't have haters, then you ain't doing your job.

"What's up, Mynique? Nice dress," I said, looking her up and down. "Isn't that from the new collection at Target?"

She put her hands on her hips and wiggled her neck. "Whatever, Maya." She held her hand up as if she was blowing me off, before turning to J. "What's up, J?" she said, smiling flirtatiously.

"It's all good," he said. Either he was blind and dumb, or he was just trying to ignore her, but he was acting like he couldn't tell she was flirting with him.

"How have you been?" Mynique smiled again as she fingered his chest and my eyebrows rose.

"I'm cool." J. Love stepped away from her. "Um, hey, babe, I'm going to go ahead and get that drink," he said, making a hasty exit. Guess he wasn't so dumb after all.

"Anything else I can help you with?" I finally told Mynique, when she just stood there all in my personal space. She was messing up my good mood.

"No, I just thought I'd come over and say hello," she said with an attitude, then flashed a big smile. "You know, while I'm waiting on my boo."

"Okay, but why don't you go wait on your *boo* somewhere else?" I said, turning back to look out on the dance floor.

"You know you're always asking for the scoop—maybe you'll want this one," she said.

As if I'd want anything Mynique Foxx had to offer.

"Mynique, if it involves you, I'm good," I told her, not even bothering to look her way.

She ignored me and kept talking. "I just thought you'd like to know that Demond Cash and I are an item," she said proudly.

That made me do a double take. *Demond Cash—the A-list actor?* What he wanted with her D-list behind was beyond me, but I wasn't going to let her see that I was fazed.

"Okay, good for you," I finally replied. "When you become somebody who is worthy of being talked about on my show, I'll look into that. Until then, later." I stood and pushed her aside. If she wouldn't leave, I would. I motioned for Mann, the security guard whom the station had hired to guard me from crazed fans, to follow me out. I'd made the mistake of getting rid of Mann at one point, but since my star had risen, I'd had stalkers, maniacs who'd wanted to hurt me, and disgruntled celebrities who'd threatened me. So, while I still didn't like Mann following me everywhere, I definitely didn't go out to clubs and parties now without him.

He led me out of the VIP area and stayed by my side as I walked around the club to see if I could spot Kennedi. I couldn't believe that she had just up and disappeared. I also needed to see if I could roll up on some dirt. I was always in gossip girl mode, and since this party had everybody who was anybody, I was bound to find some dirt up in here.

I saw one of my old friends and went to talk to her for a few minutes, and then decided that I needed to get back to the VIP because being down here with the common folk wasn't cutting it. I made my way back up the stairs and had just rounded the corner when I saw J. Love and Mynique deep in conversation.

"What's going on?" I said, approaching them. J. Love jumped back, but Mynique let out a smile.

"Just sitting here, catching up," she replied.

I looked at him and crossed my arms. If he told me he used to date Mynique Foxx, I'd be too done.

"So, you're going to give me a call sometime?" Mynique asked him.

"Uh, nah, I'm good." J. looked nervous as he rubbed the back of his neck.

I couldn't help it; I stepped in her face. "Really, Mynique? Like seriously, you want to go there?" I told her.

"My, does the little girl feel threatened by a real woman?" she sneered.

I didn't know how old Mynique was. The tabloids said she was twenty-five, but I'd bet a hundred dollars she was at least thirty-five.

"I would never be threatened by your desperate behind."
I usually didn't do any arguing over a guy. Period. But Mynique
had rubbed me the wrong way.

"Rawr," she said, making a clawing motion in my direction. "Sounds like the cat is jealous."

"Jealous of you? Get real," I snapped.

This party was definitely becoming whack. Now that I
knew they'd let Mynique Foxx into VIP, it was changing my
perspective on everything.

We stared at each other as Demond approached us. "Yo,
what's up?" he said. "Is something wrong?" He looked back
and forth between the two of us. "Hey. Maya Morgan?" he
said, recognizing me. "What's going on?" He stuck his arm
out to shake my hand. I didn't take it as I kept my eyes on
Mynique.

Demond's gaze shifted back and forth between us as we
glared at each other.

"Okay, what's up?" he asked, dropping his arm.

"Your date is what's up," I said, still not taking my eyes off
of her. This one-hit wonder was about to learn I was not the
one to mess with.

Demond put his arm around her and pulled her close.
"What is my girl over here doing?"

"You need to get *your girl* before she gets slapped," I said.
I was never one for violence, but I wasn't about to be played
either, especially when I'm sure someone around us was
rolling on his camera phone. Besides, I'm not going to lie, having Mann around gave me a little juice because he was good at
his job and he'd break up any fight before it even jumped off.

"Oh, who's going to slap me?" Mynique asked, stepping
closer to me.

"Disrespect me again and see," I replied, watching out of
the corner of my eye to make sure Mann was moving in. He
was. "You know J. Love is here with me and you got one more

time to roll up on him . . ." I wasn't even into J. Love like that, but I could just see the headline. MYNIQUE PUNKS MAYA. No ma'am.

"Yo, hold up. What?" Demond said, dropping his arm from around her neck and stepping back to stare at her. "What do you mean, roll up on your man?"

"Nothing, baby," Mynique said, pulling his arm. She no longer looked all big and bad. She actually looked . . . I don't know . . . scared.

"No, what is she talking about?" he asked, jerking his arm away.

"I'm talking about your girl right here flirting with my date, trying to get his number so they can go out, while you and me are just across the room." I turned my lips up in her direction. Yes, I'd just cold busted her.

"What?" Mynique acted shocked. "I didn't do that!" She turned to him. "Babe, she's just running her mouth. Don't listen to her."

Demond's happy demeanor had disappeared and he looked burning mad. He didn't say a word as he grabbed her arm and pulled her out of the VIP and toward the back.

J. Love just stood there like he didn't know what to say or do. Kennedi, whom I hadn't even seen approach, leaned over and said, "You think you should've done that?"

I side-eyed her. "Girl, please. In the words of Kevin Hart, she gon' learn today," I said, before picking up my bottled water and returning to my seat.

Chapter 2

It was time to call it a night. Mynique had ruined the whole mood and I hadn't even been able to enjoy myself the past twenty minutes. J. Love was trying his best to get me to go to some after-party with him. But I was a little salty with him because while he hadn't encouraged Mynique, he'd done nothing to shut her down. That wasn't a good move for him. He was already on my bad side because of the way we'd broken up. He'd treated me like crap when somebody had told him that I'd leaked something to the press. Turns out it had been a hacker/stalker, but the fact that he hadn't even given me the benefit of the doubt had severely damaged our relationship. Every time I tried to give him another chance, he did something like this to make me mad. But I couldn't deny the fact that J. Love was all that and then some. Not to mention the fact that his record was the hottest joint in the country right now. Still, I'd blessed him with my presence enough for one night.

"You ready to go?" I asked Kennedi.

"Yeah," she said. She claimed that she'd been on the dance floor all night, which was why she'd been MIA. But I didn't know if I believed her. She'd been in a foul mood most of the evening. I think it had something to do with her new boyfriend, Kendrick. Even though she kept denying it, she'd really wanted to go out with him tonight since she'd just gotten back in town. K, as I called her sometimes, had been living in Orlando, but her dad's job had transferred him back to Miami so she'd moved back two weeks ago. Personally, I'd thought she'd be upset about having to leave school her senior year, but she was happy to be back near me and Kendrick, whom she had been dating for the past month.

Tonight, though, Kendrick had had to go out of town, so Kennedi had been "stuck hanging out with me." When she told me that, I straight gave her the side eye. Nobody had to be *stuck* doing anything with me. It was a privilege to be with Maya Morgan. But since she was my BFF and I knew she was mad at Kendrick, I let her make it.

Kennedi and I had been friends since we were little. Our mothers had been friends for years. Even when she'd moved to Orlando, we'd hung out as much as possible. She had been there through every guy I'd ever dated—from my first boyfriend to my last.

"Yeah, let's go," Kennedi said, standing up from the seat she'd been plopped in for the past fifteen minutes.

I said good-bye to J. and promised to call him later. He wanted me to wait so he could walk me out, but his manager wanted him to meet some bigwig at MTV and I didn't feel like waiting. Besides, I had Mann with me.

"I still can't believe they had a party with no valet parking," I said as I thought about the two-block trek we had to pick up my car. "Where they do that at?" I moaned.

"I can go get it," Mann offered.

I probably needed the exercise because I had missed my Pilates class this week so I sucked it up, and said, "Naw, we're good."

"Well, let's go," Mann said. I debated sending him on home,

but I'd learned my lesson. The last time I'd done that, some creep had assaulted me in the mall bathroom.

Kennedi and I joked about some of the people at the party as we were walking. Mann stayed just a few feet behind us, close enough to stay on top of things, but far enough to give us our privacy.

We had just rounded the corner when Kennedi stopped and grabbed my arm. "Isn't that your girl?" she said, pointing.

I looked to the right and saw Mynique and Demond deep in conversation, and he did *not* look happy. In fact, he leaned in front of her and jabbed his finger in her face.

"Whoa," Kennedi said, pulling me back so they couldn't see us.

"Oh, dang!" I replied as I fumbled to get my iPhone out of my clutch. Mynique and Demond were going at it. Oh, I was definitely about to record this. Now that iPhones were in high definition, we could easily use this video on my show. I stepped to the side and zoomed in as much as the camera would go as the two of them argued.

"Miss Maya," Mann said, in his warning voice. But I shot him a look. He knew that I had a job to do—shoot, it was what kept his pockets fat—so he usually let me do my job with no interference.

We strained, trying to listen.

"Dang, I wish I could hear what they are saying," Kennedi whispered.

"Shh!" I motioned toward her. I didn't need any extra noise in my video. But I did slither along the wall just a little bit until I got to a point where I could hear better.

"You got me messed up!" Demond screamed. That definitely was loud enough for us to hear. It was what happened next that almost made me drop my phone. He hauled off and hit Mynique so hard it sent her tumbling to the ground. He then reached down, picked her up by her hair, and slammed her up against the wall.

While I desperately wanted to keep filming, this was one thing I couldn't stand—a guy putting his hands on a girl. So, I knew that I needed to step in.

"Hey, what's going on?" I asked, stepping around the corner.

Demond glared at Mynique, but did release her, and she scrambled to pull herself together.

"Is everything all right?" I asked, walking up to them.

"What's up, Maya? I was just having words with my girl," Demond said.

"Are you all right?" I asked, looking at Mynique.

Mynique cut her eyes at me. "Why don't you mind your own business?" she snapped, trying to brush all the dirt off her blouse. "Oh, I forgot, your janky behind doesn't know how."

"Wow," I replied, my eyes fluttering in shock. "I'm over here trying to keep you from getting your behind beat and you want to snap on me?"

"Like I said, don't worry about what's going on over here," she said, glaring at me like I was the one who had just Floyd Mayweathered her behind.

I couldn't believe this chick. I actually had to stop and do a double take, then make sure I wasn't being Punk'd. Finally, when I saw she was dead serious, I threw my hands up.

"I hope he beats the crap out of you," I said, before turning and stomping off.

Kennedi turned and took off after me. Mann was right behind her.

"She's lucky I don't fight," I huffed. "Because I'd knock her in the other side of her jaw."

"Calm down," Kennedi said. "They're just having beef. That's all."

I shook my head as we neared my car. I was still fuming.

"You all right?" Mann asked me after I unlocked my car door. He'd parked right next to me.

"Yeah, yeah, I'm fine," I barked.

He nodded and got in his car. He kept his eyes on me

while I continued venting. I knew he wouldn't leave until I drove off, but I was too mad right about now.

"See, I was trying to help her and I wasn't going to use the video, but the way she just acted, you better believe you're going to see this on *Rumor Central* first thing Monday morning," I told Kennedi.

"Maybe you shouldn't do that," Kennedi said. "No, in fact, I know you shouldn't do that. You don't want to put her business out there like that."

I stopped and stared at her. Since when was *she* the one trying to worry about someone's feelings, especially someone like Mynique Foxx?

"Really, K?" I said. "Did you not just see the way she acted toward me? And this was *after* she tried to push up on my man earlier."

"You said yourself, you don't even like J. Love like that."

I stood with the driver's-side door open. Kennedi was on the other side of the car.

"She totally disrespected me," I said.

"So? It's not like you're in some gang or something. Who cares if she disrespected you? I'm just saying, leave it alone." She got in the car and closed the door.

I looked at my friend and raised an eyebrow. Yeah, Kendrick had her all messed up because there's no way the Kennedi I knew would ever have let something like that go.

I got in as well, waved to Mann to let him know I was good, and pulled out into the main street in front of the club as Mann went the other direction.

"So you don't have a problem with him hitting her like that?" I asked Kennedi as we pulled up to the red light down the street from the club.

"All I'm saying is, that's their business," Kennedi replied. "You should just . . ." She stopped speaking in midsentence as her gaze went out the window and across the parking lot on my side.

I turned to see what she was staring at, but there was no one there but a guy and girl cuddled up against a black Escalade.

Kennedi squinted in their direction, then mumbled, "Oh, I don't think so." Before I knew anything, she threw open the car door and darted off across the street.

"Kennedi!" I quickly pulled over into the parking lot and jumped out as well. "Kennedi," I repeated. "Where are you going? What's going on?" I yelled, scurrying to catch up with her.

She didn't say anything as she stomped across the parking lot like a girl on a mission. I had no idea what had my BFF in a rage, but I kept after her, determined to find out.

Chapter 3

As I got a little closer, I could see what had lit a fire under Kennedi. Leaned up against a black Escalade, his arms around the waist of some girl with blond micro braids and an inflated butt, was Kennedi's man, Kendrick. The two of them had met at a party a few months ago. Kennedi usually didn't give guys the time of day—she'd had her heart broken in tenth grade, so she wasn't trying to go down that road again. That was why I'd been surprised when she'd told me that she and Kendrick were officially a couple. But the first time I'd seen him, I'd understood why. Ol' boy had it going on. He was fresh to death, six feet tall, light butterscotch skin, with mad swag. Think a taller, buffer Drake. And I'm talking rapper Drake, not *Degrassi* Drake. So, I got why he would be the one she'd say yes to, but Kendrick gave her the blues. He made Kennedi crazy, and I didn't like seeing my girl so strung out.

Like now. We were classy chicks. We didn't go off on dudes in public like some hood rats, yet that's exactly what Kennedi was doing.

"Are you kidding me?" Kennedi screamed, stomping over toward them.

"Kennedi," Kendrick said, pushing the girl away as he jumped back.

I wanted to tell him he was cold busted so there was no need to act like he hadn't been doing what we'd both seen him doing.

"I—I . . ."

"I nothing!" Kennedi snapped as she mushed his face. "I thought you were supposed to be out of town?"

"I—I—I . . ." he stammered, unable to complete his sentence.

The girl finally spoke up. "Um, Kendrick, do you want to tell me what's going on?"

"Nobody is talking to you!" Kennedi screamed.

"Excuse me?" the girl said, wiggling her head and going into true sistagirl mode.

"Don't talk! This ain't about you!" Kennedi put a hand up to shut her up. I couldn't believe it, but the girl actually got quiet.

Kendrick actually looked like he was trembling. "Yeah, see, um, no—I was, um, I was supposed to go, and what had happened was . . ."

I crossed my arms and stared at him. Anytime a dude starts talking about "what had happened," you know he's about to tell a lie. Kennedi thought that I didn't really cut for Kendrick because they spent so much time together, which meant we spent even less time together. But it wasn't that at all. I felt like he was a player. I had warned Kennedi of that, but she said I didn't have any proof. I had proof now and I wondered how she was going to play this out. Whether he was a cheater or not, though, my main reason for not feeling Kendrick was because he had Kennedi's nose wide open. I had never seen my girl so head over heels for a boy.

"No, babe," Kendrick said, taking a step toward her. "It ain't even like that. I just . . . this is just . . . Um, this is, um, this is my friend, uh . . ."

"Bambi," the girl said, folding her arms and getting an attitude again.

"Your mama really named you after a deer?" I couldn't help but ask.

She rolled her eyes but turned back to Kendrick. "Yeah, Bambi"—she sucked her teeth—"the chick Kendrick was just about to take back to his place. Are we still going?" she asked with major attitude.

"Your place?" Kennedi shouted. "Where are your parents?"

"Parents?" Bambi said, shocked as she swung her micro braids. "You live with your parents?"

"Yeah, since he's just nineteen!" Kennedi snapped, glaring at Kendrick like she wanted to kill him.

"Ugh!" Bambi said, like she was utterly disgusted. "You told me you were twenty-three. Punk." She stormed off, and for a minute, Kendrick really looked like he wanted to go after her.

I was just about to tell Kendrick that he was a no-good, lying dog, when next thing I knew, Kennedi hauled off and smacked him. I'm talking straight across the face, slapped him like a scene out of a movie.

"You lying piece of crap!" she said as she hit him again and again. He put his hands up to block her.

"Get off me!" he yelled.

I was stunned so I didn't move immediately, but when she started kicking him, I jumped on my girl and pulled her back.

"K, chill!" I said. "Have you lost your mind? What are you doing?"

By that time, several people had looked our way and had started making their way over, and I knew what that meant. They'd have their phones out and recording.

"You need to chill out!" I said, pulling her away. "What are you doing?"

"I trusted you!" Kennedi ignored me as she jerked free and screamed at Kendrick, kicking him and hitting him again.

I managed to grab her again and pull her back because I was surprised he had just protected himself and hadn't hauled off and hit her back. I didn't believe a guy should ever hit a girl, but I also didn't believe a girl should hit a guy. And no one could say anything if he turned around and knocked Kennedi out, because she was really out of order. I struggled to drag her away, stunned by how she was acting. I finally managed to get her to the car as she continued screaming and crying.

"Are you for real?" I said, once I had pushed her into the car.

She sat there, mad, her arms folded, her chest heaving up and down. "He is such a liar!" she cried.

"Okay, he's a liar, but did that mean you needed to jump him?"

"I didn't hurt him!" she snapped. She turned and stared out the window. "I can't believe him!" Tears were streaming down her face. I'd never seen my girl act like this.

I sat there for a moment, shock setting in. "Wow!" I said. "Kennedi, what's really going on?"

She rolled her eyes and simply said, "Can you just take me home, Maya? I'm not in the mood to talk."

I wanted to push her some more, find out what in the world had made her flip out, but I think I was too stunned. So I just started the car and slowly backed away.

Chapter 4

I had no words to explain last night. After I dropped Kennedi off at home, I spent the night tossing and turning in my own bed, trying to fall asleep. I was having a hard time because I was trying to make sense of that madness at the club last night. I'd known Kennedi since the third grade and I had never seen her act like that over a guy. I'd seen her get mad a few times, but nothing like that.

It made no sense, but I knew I needed to let it go. I needed to focus. I had a test in first period that I had to do well on, so I couldn't be worried about my girl's love life.

I threw my chemistry book in my locker just as my other BFF, Sheridan, walked up. Sheridan was the daughter of the legendary Glenda Matthews, who was probably the hottest singer/actor in Hollywood. She had like a million Grammys and several big-time movie roles and was always traveling overseas or staying at their Los Angeles home. Ms. Matthews wanted to keep Sheridan away from the glitz of Hollywood, so she kept my BFF in Miami with some of their family, who were supposed to keep an eye on her. Notice I said *supposed*, because those shiesty relatives just took Ms. Matthew's money

and let Sheridan run free. That was perfectly fine with
Sheridan though. No adult supervision meant that she
pretty much did what she wanted. She loved not having to
answer to anyone. Good thing she had a good head on her
shoulders so she stayed out of trouble. Well, major trouble,
anyway.

"Hey, how was the party last night?" she asked.

"Girl, you don't even want to know." I closed my locker
and turned toward her. A few months ago, Sheridan and I
hadn't even been speaking. We'd fallen out because Sheridan
had pushed up on my then-boyfriend, Bryce. She had been
mad over the cancellation of the *Miami Divas* and all the
drama afterward. So, since I knew she'd just been trying to be
dirty, and she'd truly apologized, I'd forgiven her.

"I tried to call you last night," I said to Sheridan. "It went
straight to your voice mail."

"Yeah, my phone was dead and my charger wasn't working," she replied. "But what's up? Tell me about the party."

I shook my head. Lately, Sheridan always had an excuse
for why she couldn't call or hang out. I began replaying the
night. "The party was cool. It was tight, seriously. But it's
what happened after the party that's not making sense to me."
I stopped and turned to face her. "It's Kennedi. She went ballistic."

"What do you mean?"

I needed to hurry up and tell her what had happened before we saw Kennedi. "Kennedi was seriously trippin'," I continued. "I'm talking, I'm trying to figure out if she was on
some kind of drugs because of the way she was trippin'."

Sheridan and I walked past a group of students who were
dragging up the walkway, late as well. We attended the presti-
gious private Miami High School, and because of all the
money our parents paid for us to go here, the teachers often
cut us slack when it came to things like punctuality. Since I

started hosting *Rumor Central*, though, I'd been pushing my luck. Not only was I late almost daily, my grades were plummeting because I barely had time for anything outside of the show. I'd been trying to get my academic act together since my mom threatened to make me quit my show if I didn't get my grades up, as if that would really happen. Even still, I wasn't trying to flunk out of my senior year, so I'd been trying to get my grades up because there was nothing cute about being dumb.

I'd given up on the whole tutor thing because I hadn't had much luck with that. The last two tutors I'd had had turned out to be psychopaths (long story). Now I was just trying to do it myself.

"So what are you talking about, she went ballistic? Hurry up and tell me before the bell rings," Sheridan said.

I actually looked around for Kennedi just to make sure she didn't pop up on us.

"Apparently, Kennedi thought Kendrick—"

"That's her new boyfriend, right?"

"Yeah," I continued. "Apparently, she thought he was going out of town, but he wasn't. He lied to her and was at the party hugged up with another girl."

"What? For real?" Sheridan said.

While we walked, I told Sheridan everything about how we'd caught Kendrick with Bambi and how Kennedi had ended up losing her dang mind.

We stopped in front of my first-period classroom.

"So, I was trying to figure out what made her—" Before I could finish talking, Sheridan's boyfriend, Javier Espinosa, walked up, and I couldn't help but groan. While I didn't particularly care for Kendrick, I downright hated Javier. He was one of the scholarship kids—students who couldn't afford to come here but were given a scholarship by some charitable foundation. He and Sheridan had been kicking it for the last month. I wasn't feeling it at all because Javier was the rudest, most disrespectful guy I had ever seen, and I couldn't for the life of me see why Sheridan liked him. Yes, he was cute. Real cute. And yes, he was fine. Real fine. He reminded me of Mario Lopez without the dimples. But he was still rude and nasty to people. Not Sheridan, though. For some reason, he treated Sheridan like a queen. At least according to her, he did. In the beginning I *had* seen him putting her on a pedestal, but the last week or so, he'd been talking to her like she'd been downgraded to servant.

"Hey, baby," Sheridan said as he approached us.

"Hey, babe," he replied, leaning in and kissing her.

"Is 'babe' the only one you see standing here?" I asked.

He looked at me, looked back at her, and said, "Yeah."

"Javier." Sheridan giggled, although I didn't see what was funny. "You said you were going to start being nice to my friends."

He laughed and then looked back at me. "What's up, Millie?"

"Really?" I said as I rolled my eyes.

"See, babe? Trying to be nice to her and she still has a stank attitude," he said.

"Because you know my name isn't Millie, idiot."

"I wish you two would learn to get along," Sheridan interrupted. She had a better chance of Nicki Minaj and Mariah Carey becoming BFFs.

"I'm trying to be nice. You see she's calling me names," Javier said, grinning like he was some kind of comedian.

I threw my hands up. It didn't even do any good to talk to Sheridan about guys. I had tried to tell her when she was dating my cousin a few months ago. I'd tried to tell her *then* that my cousin was no good. I loved Travis, and he was super cute with a dimpled smile that the girls went crazy over, but he was no good when it came to the girls. I'd told Sheridan that dating him would only get her heart broken, but she hadn't been trying to hear it and that's exactly what had happened. She'd found out Travis had cheated on her and it had dang near busted up our friendship. If I told her that about my own blood and she didn't listen, why would I expect her to listen now?

"So, um, are we going to finish talking?" I asked Sheridan. I didn't even bother looking at that jerk. I wished he would just disappear.

Javier didn't give her a chance to answer. "Nah, she's going with me. She's going to walk with me to her next class."

"So, now he's speaking for you?" I told Sheridan.

"You know what, Maya?" Javier said. "How about you try to get your own man and stop sabotaging your friends? Or are you jealous of Sheridan?" He put his arm around Sheridan's neck and pulled her close. "Yeah, babe. I think that's what it is," Javier said, looking me up and down. "She's hatin' because you all happy and boo'd up."

"Are you freaking insane?" I said, finally acknowledging that fool. "Maya Morgan isn't jealous of anyone," I told him. "Especially not because she has you! I'm sure if I wanted a scholarship thug from the other side of the tracks, I could get one, too."

"Maya!" Sheridan said. How was she gonna try to check me and not that buster boyfriend of hers?

He lost a little of his smile. "Nah, babe. It's cool. That's what people do when they're hatin' on you."

"Ugh, I'm not hating on my BFF. Get real."

"Yeah, about that whole BFF thing," he said with a smirk. "We gots to give you your walking papers." He leaned in and tongue kissed Sheridan right there in the hall. It was so disgusting. "I'm her new BFF," Javier said, after pulling away from her.

She giggled like that mess was actually funny, and I wanted to throw up in my mouth.

"Whatever," I said, turning and stomping into my class-room. I don't know if it was something in the air or what, be-cause both of my girls had gone completely berserk. Believe me, I wasn't a hater, but I hated the way both of my girls were acting!

Chapter 5

It seemed like this meeting had been going on forever. I glanced down at my watch. We'd already been in this freezing conference room for more than an hour, and that was after I'd had to spend seven freakin' hours at school. I was absolutely exhausted and the last place I wanted to be was sitting up in a stupid meeting. I hated these quarterly planning meetings, and if there had been any kind of way I could've skipped out on it, I would have. But Tamara had personally sent me a text, reminding me to be there, then had my producer, Dexter, meet me at my office to walk me to the meeting room. Tamara was my boss, though I'd first met her because she was a friend of my family. The way she was tripping with me lately sometimes made me wonder if she had forgotten that.

The first half of the meeting had been a bunch of boring numbers stuff, and the second half, the part they were doing now, well, I really wasn't looking forward to that because I knew, at some point, all eyes were going to be on me.

"So, we got the Kevin Young story locked down," Tamara said after the producer handling that story finished giving her report. There were six people at the meeting: me, Tamara,

Dexter, an associate producer, one of Tamara's assistants and someone from the corporate office.

Tamara turned to one of her assistants—she had like five. "Sonia, were you able to find anything more about that drama with Paul Harrington?"

The geeky-looking girl fumbled through some papers. "Yes," she said, pulling out whatever she had been looking for. "Apparently, his ex filed a restraining order and she's shopping a reality show."

Tamara gave Dexter a side eye, which only meant that he'd be calling her about that reality show as soon as this meeting was over.

"Okay, great." And the moment I had been dreading since I'd stepped foot in this meeting finally arrived as Tamara turned to me. "Maya, what do you have? It's been a minute since you had some good stuff."

"Right," Dexter chimed in. "We need some more Bling Ring, cheerleader-escort-type stories."

"Don't forget the Glenda Matthews story," an assistant producer named Ken added. "That had to be the all-time best."

They all nodded in agreement at that. That may have been an all-time best for them, but it had to be the story that I regretted the most.

When I'd first started doing *Rumor Central* and gotten really mad at Sheridan, I'd found out that her mom had had a baby before Sheridan and had given the child up for adoption so it wouldn't mess up her career. I'd run the story on my show. I know, janky. But to my defense, Sheridan had done some low-down, dirty stuff as well. Like sending out a sexy lingerie pic I had texted Bryce. She'd sent it to everyone in his contact list. And let's not forget the fact that she'd messed with him in the first place, so, as far as I was concerned, that was war.

But I'd ended up being the good one in all of that mess

because Sheridan had been able to find out about a sister that she'd never known that she had. To this day, she kept in touch with Valerie. Valerie's adoptive parents didn't want them talking and had moved her away, but Sheridan stayed hopeful that once they got older, they could reconnect. And that was all thanks to me.

"Hello," Tamara said, snapping me out of my thoughts.

"Oh, yeah, yeah," I said, turning my attention back to the meeting. "What did you say?"

Tamara looked at me sternly. "I said, what do you have, Maya?"

I looked down at my phone and the video of Demond and Mynique. "Umm, I'm working on some stuff," I said. I couldn't believe I was torn over whether to air the video of Demond and Mynique. Oh, believe me, I wanted to. But Kennedi had really pleaded with me not to. If I didn't know better, I would've thought that Mynique had put her up to it. But she'd said she felt sorry for Mynique being in an abusive situation.

Rumor Central had made a name for itself (well, I made a name for *Rumor Central*) by putting the rumors out there, then letting people draw their own conclusions. My show was like Perez Hilton, MediaTakeOut, and Bossip on TV—but from a teen perspective. And while that was only part of the show (the other was the celebrities coming on, talking about what's hot in their lives, addressing some of the gossip that's going on out there about them, stuff like that), the Rumor Mill, which is what we'd started calling the section of the show where I dished dirt, was the most popular part of the show.

"Come on, Maya," Tamara said, snapping her fingers in my face. "Are you even here with us today?"

"Yeah, yeah," I said, trying to figure out why my mind kept drifting off. Probably because I was tired and ready to go home.

"Are you getting soft, losing your touch?" Dexter asked.

"Never that," I said, shifting in my chair as I tried to compose myself.

"Maya, in all seriousness, this is no joke. Yes, the ratings are good, but they could be better. We used to blow the competition out of the water. Now, we barely beat them."

I wanted to tell her, "But we are beating them." But I knew that wouldn't be good enough for Tamara, so I stayed quiet.

"Maya, we need some hard stuff," Tamara added.

Dexter cleared his throat. "Well, what about that stuff I heard about your boy getting some drug charges?"

I glared at Dexter and his red mop-head self. He was getting as bad as Tamara. No, he was worse than Tamara. "First of all," I began, "J. Love is not my boy. Second of all, someone on his tour bus was caught with marijuana. He wasn't. And third, unless it's major, I don't want to touch any story about J. Love."

Dexter glared right back at me. He hated for me to have any kind of personal feelings about stories that we aired.

"Now, now," Tamara said, stepping in. "Maya's right. It's a dope charge. And it's not even J. Love, so it's not worth it." She turned to me. "But Maya, we need you to get on it. We did the whole Cancun spring break thing, and you came back with nothing."

"And yes, you busted the K2 ring, but you ended up becoming the story," Dexter added. "We need more."

"Fine, I am looking into a tip about Demond Cash and Mynique Foxx," I said, reluctantly.

Their eyes grew big. "The actor Demond Cash?" Dexter asked, excitement already building.

I nodded. "Yeah. I think he may be abusive, but I'm checking my sources right now."

Chatter filled the room. "Oooh, that would be good," Tamara said. "Definitely keep us posted on that."

I nodded, grateful when Tamara started wrapping up the meeting. As I headed back to my office, I couldn't help but wonder, was Dexter right? Why was I even second-guessing whether to run that story? Was I going soft? Was I getting a conscience?

I opened the door and walked into my office/dressing room. My assistant, Yolanda, was sitting at the small conference table going over some paperwork.

"Hey, where'd these come from?" I said, leaning over and sniffing the big bouquet of roses that sat on my desk.

"Oh, the front desk brought those back about twenty minutes ago," she said.

"Who are they from?"

"Who knows?" she replied. "Probably one of your many admirers."

I plucked the card out. I did have a lot of admirers, but since you never knew who was crazy and who wasn't, I tried to steer clear of those people. I smiled when I read the card. "It's from Alvin."

"Of course it is." Yolanda chuckled. She was a great assistant who stayed out of my business, but Alvin was always sending me sweet little gifts, so she knew about him. Alvin was just a really good friend, though. We'd met through a friend of Kennedi's who had hooked me up with him to help me try and track down this crazed fan who was stalking me. Alvin was like a computer genius. But as most geniuses were, he was a stone-cold nerd. And although he'd ended up being a great guy, Maya Morgan didn't do nerds. Still, we talked on the phone almost every day and joked all the time. Though I really liked having him as a friend and I knew he wanted to take our relationship to the next level, he never pressured me or made me feel uncomfortable, so we stayed good friends.

" 'Congratulations on another ratings win,' " I said, reading the card.

I hadn't even told Alvin that the ratings had come in and *Rumor Central* had won its time slot in thirty-three markets. But it didn't surprise me that he knew.

I picked up the phone and dialed Alvin's number. "Hey, you," I said when he picked up the phone.

"Hey, gorgeous," he replied.

"Got the flowers."

"Good. I know how much you love white lilies."

"They are beautiful. How did you know about the ratings?" I asked.

"I knew they came out today, so I went and checked, even though I already knew they were going to be good."

"You wouldn't know they were good the way my bosses are trippin'," I said, falling back in my desk chair.

"That's because they're trying to hang on to the top spot. The minute you become complacent, someone snatches your crown."

"No worries. This crown is positioned tightly on my head."

He laughed. "Of course it is. Is everything else okay?"

I nodded as Yolanda motioned that she was leaving. As soon as she left, I loudly exhaled. "No. Everything is not okay. My girls are losing their doggone minds," I said.

"Boy trouble?"

"How'd you guess?" I asked.

"Because your girls have good heads on their shoulders and only one thing can send a girl over the edge like that—a boy."

"You ain't never lied," I replied. "They are definitely over the edge. Now the question is, can I reel them back in before it's too late?"

Chapter 6

My cousin was the ultimate playa. He was standing next to his car (a shiny red Camaro that my dad had bought him when he moved here). He looked like he should've been shooting a rap video or something, he was in such serious mack mode.

These girls were acting like Travis was still brand new to our school. Travis was from Brooklyn, New York. Growing up, we used to be really tight. We were close in age—he was only a few months older than me, and was the brother I never had. He'd come to live with us three months ago after some drama at home, but he was still pulling in girls like he was fresh meat. The jacked-up part was most of them knew that he had cheated on Sheridan with Angel, dumped Angel for Tonya, and kicked Tonya to the curb for Vanessa. But these girls were thirsty and didn't care. Probably because Travis was easily one of the hottest guys at Miami High. He was Trey Songz fine, with smooth chocolate skin and a body that looked like he worked out religiously, although he didn't. Add to that the fact that he had a little bad-boy swag and a slamming personality, and I'd known these chicks were going to be all over him the moment he stepped on campus. And they had been.

"Travis, can you pull yourself away from your groupie for a minute?" I said, approaching him.

Vanessa rolled her eyes at me. The bootleg girls my cousin messed with weren't even in the same zip code as me, so I never gave them the time of day, even though they tried to befriend me just to get close to him. And Vanessa had to be bottom of the barrel. She always dressed like she needed to be doing one of those dollar-a-minute webcam videos. Like now, she had on some see-through leggings and a too-little sequined top. She looked like she was going to the club, not to school.

"What's up, Cuz?" Travis pulled a piece of paper out of his back pocket and held it up. "I got an A-plus on my history paper."

Ugh, Travis made me so sick. He'd started on that paper at eight o'clock, the night before it was due. By ten, he was done. And he'd gotten an A-plus. I'd worked on mine off and on for three weeks and I'd still gotten a C. Life could be so unfair.

I pushed his paper away. "Whatever. Have you seen Sheridan?"

That made Vanessa's eyebrows rise and she shot me a funky look.

"Why would I have seen Sheridan?" he asked.

"Yeah, why would he have seen Sheridan?" Vanessa echoed.

"Why is nobody talking to you?" I told her. She'd been with Travis for all of two days. She needed to disappear from my presence. Like yesterday.

I turned back to Travis. "I was supposed to meet Sheridan after school and I can't find her and she's not answering her phone."

"Well, I haven't seen her." Travis shrugged as he rolled his essay up and put it in his back pocket.

"Dang." I looked around. "She has my chemistry work-sheet and she was supposed to be meeting me after school to give it to me. She can't be gone since her car is still here." I pointed to her silver Benz that sat across the parking lot.

"Well, she ain't here," Vanessa said. She had this irritated look on her face like I was really messing with her groove.

"Well, where is she then?"

Vanessa shrugged nonchalantly. "Javier dragged her off, grabbed her by her hair and threw her in some raggedy car his homeboy was driving."

Travis's eyes bugged in shock. "He did what?"

Vanessa immediately got an attitude, wiggling her neck as she said, "And why do you care?"

"Because I don't believe in a dude putting his hands on a girl." Travis frowned, like what Vanessa had just said was registering in his brain. I hadn't told him about Javier being disrespectful, so as far as he knew, Sheridan and Javier were cool.

Before Travis and Sheridan decided to mess up things by being boyfriend-girlfriend, they'd been just good friends. When we were little and Travis would spend summers with my family, the three of us had been inseparable. So, I knew that he wouldn't be happy to hear the news about Javier manhandling her. "You gotta be pretty lame to be laying hands on a girl," he growled.

That made Vanessa smile. "Aww, you so sweet."

I rolled my eyes. "Where were they going?" I asked her.

She shook her head, not bothering to hide her irritation. "I don't know. They were arguing. He didn't hit her or nothing. He just pushed her and was talking to her all crazy."

"Ugh," I grumbled as I pulled out my phone and punched in Sheridan's number again. It still went straight to voice mail.

I was about to say something when I saw Travis looking at his own phone funny. The expression on his face concerned me.

"Travis? What is it?"

"I just got a text. From Willie."

"Willie? Who is Willie?" I asked.

"My mom's boyfriend." He frowned as he swiped the screen on his phone. "Why is he texting me?" Then his eyes grew big.

"What? What does the text say?" I asked, peering at his screen.

Travis read from his phone. " 'Trying to get in touch with you. You need to come home. Your mom is dying.' "

"What?" I said, snatching his phone. "Who sends something like that in a text?"

Travis snatched the phone back. "Man, this dude here." His fingers quickly punched the screen, and then he put the phone to his ear.

"Yo, Willie, what's up? . . . Look, man, I didn't call you for all that. What's wrong with my mama? . . . Man, you'd better tell me what's going on with my mama!"

I snatched the phone because Travis was actually shaking. "Hello," I said.

"Who dis?" the voice replied.

"This is Maya, Travis's cousin."

I heard him grunt, then say, "Oh, the rich girl?"

"Yeah, whatever," I snapped. "What's going on with Aunt Bev?" I didn't know much about Willie. I'd just heard Travis mention him a couple of times only to say he couln't stand him.

"You need to get Daddy Warbucks to send us some money," Willie said matter-of-factly. "Bev ain't doing too good and she needs to be in a better hospital than this public dump. Then, all this medication dey got her on costin' a grip. Don't make no sense that we struggling and got bills out the ying-yang because she can't work. Your pops needs to wire us some money today because it done got get real real up here."

"What does that mean?" I said. "Speak English!"

"Look," Willie huffed, "like I said, Bev ain't doing too good. She getting sicker and they don't know if she gon' make it. I just thought Travis should know."

"Through texts, though? Really?" I said.

"Whatever. I didn't have to get in touch with him at all. I coulda just let his ol' lady croak and not even tell him. I was doing him a favor. I didn't feel like talking to that little punk anyway. I'm just trying to let him know about his mama. Do what you want with the info. But I need you to tell yo' daddy to get us some cheddar ASAP."

I sighed heavily. I knew it would be useless to argue with this man. "I'll ask my dad to call," I replied, then glanced at Travis's caller ID. "Is this your number?"

"Yeah. But don't call," Willie said. "Just send money. And tell Travis he need to get home before his mama dies." He slammed the phone down before I could say anything else. I stood there, dumbfounded. No wonder Travis couldn't stand this guy.

"What is he talking about?" Travis asked.

I didn't want to relay all of what Willie had said until my dad had a chance to confirm things. "I don't know. Let me call Dad."

Vanessa stood there while I dialed my dad's number. Finally, I said, "Can you excuse us? We have a family emergency here?"

Vanessa huffed and looked to Travis like she wanted him to tell her something different. But he just said, "Yo, I'll catch up with you later." The look on his face must've told her that it wasn't even open for discussion because she just said, "Okay, babe. Call me and let me know what's going on."

Travis didn't even acknowledge her as she walked away. He just kept staring at me. My dad's cell went to his voice mail so I called his office.

"Morgan Enterprises, this is Lorna," my dad's longtime secretary said.

"Hi, Lorna. This is Maya. Is my dad around?"

"Hi, Maya," she cheerfully replied. "I'm sorry, your dad is in a meeting."

"This is pretty important. Is there any way you can get him?"

"Ooh, the meeting he's in is with some stockholders. He specifically asked not to be disturbed," Lorna said with a worried tone. My dad ran a tight ship and I knew most of his employees were afraid of him.

"It's a family emergency, Lorna," I firmly said. "Really important."

She hesitated, then said, "Okay, okay, I'll let him know." She had me on hold a few minutes and Travis looked like he was about to bust a nerve.

"Chill," I mouthed to him. "It's probably Willie just trying to get some money. I'm sure Aunt Bev is fine." I knew my words were useless in comforting him because my own stomach was turning flips and it wasn't even my mother.

"Where is Uncle Myles?" Travis asked after a few more minutes.

"Just hold on," I said.

Finally, my dad picked up the phone. "Maya," he said. I could hear the panic in his voice.

"Yeah, Daddy."

"What's wrong, honey? Are you okay?"

"Yes, we're about to leave school and Travis just got a call from somebody named Willie, Aunt Bev's boyfriend. He told Travis Aunt Bev is dying and he needs to get home ASAP."

"What?" my dad yelled, his voice full of shock.

"Yes, and he texted that mess first. Travis is about to go crazy," I said.

"This guy here," my dad mumbled.

"Daddy, what's going on?" I asked.

He blew a frustrated breath. "I don't know, sweet pea. Let me find out. You and Travis just go on to the house. I'll meet you guys there. Tell Travis everything is going to be fine. He knows Willie is over the top."

Travis snatched the phone away from me and put it to his ear. "Unc, is my mom okay?"

I don't know what my dad was saying to him, but it obviously was enough to calm him down because his shoulders seemed to relax a little, then he said, "All right. We'll see you in a little bit." He hung up the phone and handed it back to me. "He said for us to get to the house."

My cousin didn't even wait for me as he climbed in his car and headed home.

Chapter 7

After the stress of last night, I should've stayed at home with Travis today. I never did catch up with Sheridan to get my chemistry paper so I was completely unprepared for my test today.

My dad hadn't been able to get in touch with Willie all evening. Finally, after my dad left a message, asking where he should send the money, Willie called back. Turned out, Aunt Bev was in pretty bad shape, but she wasn't dying like Willie made it seem. Still, Travis had been so upset all evening. And today, he said he wasn't even in the mood to come to school.

As soon as I rounded the corner after my third-period class, I knew I should've stayed at home with my cousin. I wanted to turn and go the other way. Bali, Evian, and Shay, were standing there, huddled in a circle. And from the way they were side-eyeing me, they were no doubt talking about me. It's like having my name in their mouth gave them life. The sad part was we all used to be cool, but that was before all the drama. Back before *Rumor Central*. Evian needed to be thanking me, though, because after that fiasco a few weeks ago where she faked her own kidnapping trying to get some notoriety I could've seriously ruined her. We were all set to put her on blast on *Rumor Central* and I nixed it. I felt sorry for her, so I took up for her on the air, explaining why she'd done it, how desperation sometimes drove people too far. I made her sympathetic. Because I played it low, the story died down and the spotlight didn't stay on her long.

So, Evian needed to be kissing my pinky toe, not talking about me. I guess she knew it because as I approached them, she kind of slithered to the back like she wanted no part of what they were about to do.

"Excuse me," I said, trying to step around Bali, who had moved his flamin' behind right in front of me to block my path. He swung his blond swoop (don't even ask) to get it out of his face. His skinny jeans looked like they were cutting off his circulation and that top looked like it had come straight off the designer's rack. Bali always did do it up big. His father was a Cuban bigwig so they had more than enough money to keep him looking fab. But, Bali had a temper that kept him in trouble.

"Hey, Diva," Bali said with a snide grin.

"What's up, Bali?" I casually replied, trying not to act irritated. The bad part is Bali and I used to be the tightest of us all (next to me and Sheridan). Like the others, he had been upset when they'd fired the *Miami Divas*. Then, he'd gotten really mad because I'd done the story on the "Bling Ring" on my show. Bali had been among several people taking part in the Bling Ring, where some of his friends broke into celebrities' homes and stole stuff. Bali didn't steal anything, but he's gone along for the thrill and so he could film it all. He'd given me one of the videos a long time ago, and well, my producers had been sweating me for some juicy gossip and it didn't get any juicier than that video. After my story, Bali's dad had been so mad that he'd sent Bali back to Cuba to live with relatives. But that hadn't lasted long and Bali was back now, so why was he hating on me?

"So, I hear you and your girls like to let boys beat up on you," Bali said. "Do you need my help?" He batted his mink eyelashes and tried to act like he was truly concerned.

I rolled my eyes. If I ever did get into a fight, Bali would've been the one I'd have wanted on my side. A couple of the jocks had made the mistake of trying to punk him sophomore year because he was so flamboyant. Even though he barely weighed a hundred and fifteen pounds, he'd beat them down so bad, it had generated more than two million views on YouTube.

Granted, Shay and I had a fight right after I got my own show, I wasn't a fighter. I was a suer. I would sue anybody who touched me. Don't get me wrong, I *could* fight. I just didn't because I was way too classy for that. Even still, I told Bali, "Sweetie, you don't ever have to worry your pretty little swoop about anybody ever putting their hands on me," I said.

"Yeah, especially Bryce," Shay said, motioning down the hall at my ex-boyfriend, Bryce Logan, who was hugged up with his girlfriend, Callie. "Looks like his hands are wrapped all around Callie these days."

Shay was hoping to get a rise out of me talking about the girl Bryce had started dating after me. Shay knew how much in love Bryce and I used to be so I guess she thought I was going to get mad. I admit (well, I wouldn't admit it out loud) I was a little shocked that Bryce and Callie were still together. It had been almost six months now. But Bryce was the past. As if that nobody or his girlfriend were even on my radar now.

"You know, I just asked because I saw Sheridan and Javier going at it earlier and I swear he was about to slap the mess out of her," Bali continued. I think they were all a little mad at Sheridan because she hadn't stayed mad at me over the *Miami Divas* thing. "Then," Bali continued, "I heard about what went down at the party with Kennedi and her boo."

"So, you know, birds of a feather," Shay added, laughing.

"So that means you're a thieving wannabe girl, too," I said bluntly.

Both her and Bali glared at me. "At least I'm not a gossiping, backstabbing tramp," she shot back.

Shay and I definitely had the most volatile of the relationships. Maybe it was because she was ghetto-rich and I didn't do ghetto. Even when we tried to move forward and at least be frenemies, we always ended up fighting again.

"Shouldn't you be somewhere raising bail money?" I asked her. "I heard your daddy got arrested last night at the strip club."

I knew it was low to talk about her dad, Jalen Turner, one of the biggest basketball players in the country and a center for the Miami Heat. Yes, he was rich, but money couldn't buy class and Mr. Turner proved that with his numerous arrests for fighting, drinking, and other stuff.

"Girl, I will knock the mess outta you," Shay said, stepping toward me.

Bali stepped in my face, blocking her. Good thing, because I was about to take some of her daddy's millions.

"Look here," Bali said, wagging a finger in my direction.

"No, you look," I said, not backing down. "I don't have a beef with you, Bali. In fact, we used to be really cool."

"*Used* to be," he said, rolling his eyes.

"All I'm saying is, I don't want the drama," I continued. "We know where we stand with each other, and I'm cool with that. I'm trying to go to class, so excuse me." I tried to step around him again, but he jumped in front of me again.

"Naw, see, you really think you're the queen bee now, but you're not."

I sighed heavily. Why they'd picked today of all days to mess with me, I didn't know. But I was tired of being nice. "Look, Bali. It's no need to hate me. Your show didn't work, but I'm sure if you guys get together"—I motioned to all of them, including Evian, who still hadn't said a word—"and get with some of the kids from the broadcasting class, I'm sure you all can film some stuff to be on YouTube."

"Is she throwing shade?" Bali asked, looking at Shay.

"It's all she knows how to do," Shay said, turning her lips out.

Thankfully, our principal, Mr. Carvin, stepped out in the hall and started yelling for us to get to class. He stopped right in front of me.

"Miss Morgan, are you causing problems again?" Mr. Carvin didn't particularly care for me because he said the stories I did "made our school look bad." But since my shine kept Miami High in the limelight, there wasn't a lot he could do about it.

"Just trying to mind my own business, Mr. Carvin," I said.

Shay and Bali coughed loudly. I ignored them and took Mr. Carvin's interruption as my cue to leave. I was done arguing with that group of losers anyway. I stepped around them and made my way down the hall.

But I couldn't help but think about what they'd said. Now, my girls' reputations were reflecting on me. I didn't let guys mistreat me, period. I dang sure wasn't about to let someone lay his hands on me. And I hated being lumped in the same category as anyone who did.

I had just made it to my seventh-period class when I saw Javier and Sheridan. And no, he wasn't mistreating her this time, but he dang sure was disrespecting her. Once again, he had his tongue down her throat. Slobbing her down, in the middle of the hallway.

"Really?" I said, approaching them.

Javier licked his lips as they looked at me while backing up from one another.

"Aww, here she come with this again," Javier said.

"Disgusting," I said, turning to Sheridan. "Don't you have more self-respect? You're really gonna let him do this in public?"

"It's called PDA. I know you don't know anything about it," Javier said. He put his arm around her. I don't know why that made me feel like he was trying to stake his claim or something. I just couldn't believe Sheridan couldn't see through this mess.

It's like Sheridan had suddenly gotten laryngitis or something around this dude. She never got a word in because he was always talking for her.

"Maya," Sheridan began. "It's not even like—"

"Nah, she ain't your mama," Javier interrupted. "You don't owe her an explanation."

"Ugh. Whatever," I said. "Sheridan, what's up? You were supposed to meet with that chemistry worksheet. I've been calling and calling."

She smiled. "Oh, girl, I am so sorry. I forgot I was supposed to be meeting you."

I could only stare at her. I was waiting for her to bust out laughing or something, because this had to be a joke.

"Seriously?"

She just stood there looking all innocent until I finally said, "So, why didn't you answer your phone all evening?"

"Oh, I had to let Javier borrow my phone yesterday," she said, like that mess was normal.

"Borrow your phone?" I yelled. "Who does that?"

"People in love," Javier answered, "something you'd know nothing about. I was in a bind and my girl helped me out by letting me use her phone."

I gave him the hand and stared at Sheridan. "He's slipping you drugs, right? I mean, that's the only explanation for how you're acting."

"Chill out, Maya. Dang," she huffed. "I don't have anything to hide. He can use my phone."

I took a deep breath. "So, I guess you didn't see the many times I called her."

Javier grinned, all stupid-looking as he hunched his shoulders. "Sorry. I didn't."

"Whatever," I said, pushing past him and into my classroom. I seriously was about to be done with Sheridan. If she was cool with that jerk, I didn't even know if I wanted her as my friend anymore!

Chapter 8

Could my BFF actually be back? The laughter filled the air in the hallway as Kennedi and I cracked jokes and ragged on our classmates. Kennedi seemed to be back to her normal, bubbly self. She was in a really good mood. Of course, I assumed that meant that her and Kendrick had made up, but honestly, I didn't even bother to ask because I really didn't want to know. The ups and downs of their relationship were enough to drive a person crazy. Besides, if we talked about him, I was going to have to tell her about herself again, and I didn't even want to go there and mess up the mood.

"Did you see that outfit Kary has on?" Kennedi said, pointing across the hall. Karrington White, or Kary as those who tortured her called her, was one of the smartest girls at Miami High. A pretty Filipino girl with short brown hair and freckles that cascaded down the bridge of her nose, she desperately wanted to be in the It Clique. And although she had enough money, (her parents were big time in the finance business), the girl was weird. She dressed funny, like someone who just flipped through all the magazines, then bought the most popular stuff and threw it together with no style or thought. She always seemed like she was trying way too hard so nobody wanted to hang out with her.

"Ewww." I took in her latest getup, a multicolor peasant skirt and ruffled shirt. "It looks like she raided the trash bins at New York fashion week," I said as we headed to my car.

I was going to drop Kennedi off at home before I went to the station. We were working on a story about Jason Richards, a married Miami Dolphins football player who got a seventeen-year-old girl pregnant.

"Why don't you come to the station and hang out on set?" I asked her. I was really enjoying having the old K back and wanted to hang out.

"Nah." She shook her head. "I always feel like I'm in the way. Plus, I don't want to just sit there all evening."

"I just have to tape. I won't be there long. Then we can go get something to eat."

"In that case, cool," she said. "It's been a minute since we just kicked it." She had just tossed her backpack into my backseat and was about to get in when we heard a honk. Both of us turned to see Kendrick's Escalade pulling into the parking lot. I lost my smile and Kennedi's grew even bigger. She didn't say a word as she bounced away from my car and over to him.

"Hey, babe," she said.

He leaned out of the truck. "What's up, beautiful?" He looked my way. "Hey, Maya."

"Hey, Kendrick" was all I could force myself to say. If he was fazed, he didn't let on.

"What are you doing here?" Sheridan asked. It was so lame how she was acting like some sixth-grader with her first crush. I wanted to grab her, shake some sense into her, and remind her about Bambi.

"I wanted to surprise you," Kendrick said, pinching her chin. "I was hoping I didn't miss you."

"You didn't."

"Well, let's go grab some grub." He motioned for her to get in on the other side of his truck.

"Cool."

I just stared at her. "Really? I thought we were going to get something to eat later."

"I'm hungry now." She reached in the backseat of my car and grabbed her bag. "I'll catch up with you later."

I just rolled my eyes and got in the car. So much for our boy code—BFFs before boys. Because both Sheridan and Kennedi had kicked me to the curb for two dudes who didn't deserve it.

I shook off thoughts of my traitor BFF and turned the radio to the hip-hop station as I made my way to the studio.

I had barely sat down at my desk thirty minutes when I looked up to see Tamara walking in.

"We had some last-minute changes," Tamara said, not even bothering to say hello. It wasn't not that she was rude. Tamara was just always in business mode. She didn't have time for little things like hello. "Jason's attorney sent over a statement," Tamara continued. "I had them include that in your report." She handed me some papers. "I wanted you to be aware of it before you got on air. The changes are reflected in your script. Look over them now."

I took the papers, set them on my vanity table, and started changing into the outfit I would be taping in today.

"All right, I'll get changed and look over it while I'm in hair and makeup," I told her.

Tamara nodded her approval. "So, have you heard anything else on the Demond-Mynique situation? Were you able to confirm if they actually physically fought?"

"No," I replied, holding up an emerald-green wrap dress and plum pantsuit that the stylists had left out for me to choose from.

"Maya," Tamara said, like she was really disappointed in me. "We really need to be making some progress on this story.

Find out what's going on. If they had a fight, were police called? Did she press charges? We can't let the ball drop on this. I mean, you pitch the story, but you keep making excuses about why you don't want to follow up. At least call, see if you can get a statement from her or Demond. We need to run something. I don't have to tell you, if this story pops up somewhere else, I am not going to be pleased."

"Fine," I said. For the first time in, like, forever, my job was getting on my nerves. "I'll get right on it," I told her.

Tamara gave me a "you'd better" look and exited my office. I chose the plum pantsuit, changed, then called Portia, the makeup artist, and told her that I was ready. While I waited, I decided to go ahead and see what I could find out about Demond and Mynique. Maybe I could do a story without running the video, because the video was pretty bad.

I didn't have Mynique's cell phone number, but I managed to find her home number online. I used the station phone to dial the number.

A woman's voice answered. "Hello."

"Hi, is Mynique Foxx available?"

There was a hesitation, and then the woman said, "This is her cousin. Mynique doesn't live here."

"Oh, well, this is Maya Morgan from—"

"Oh, my God! Maya Morgan from *Rumor Central*?" the girl squealed so loud.

"Yeah, that Maya Morgan." I smiled. I loved when people I was trying to get information from knew me. It made my job so much easier.

"Oh, my God. You are the bomb-dot-com," she continued. "I love your show. Oooh, I remember when you broke that story about—"

"Thank you so much," I said, cutting her off. I knew if I didn't, she would keep going on and on. "I was trying to get in touch with Mynique."

"For what?" The excitement quickly left her voice.

I debated how much I should say, but I needed to get some info. "Do you know how to get in touch with Mynique?"

She hesitated again, then said, "Nah, I don't."

"Are you guys close?" I decided to ask.

"Umph, depends on what you call close."

I could tell from her tone that there was some animosity there so I decided to pounce. "Well, the other day, I actually stumbled upon Mynique and her boyfriend, Demond."

"Umph," she repeated, but didn't say anything more.

"Well, they were in the middle of a pretty heated argument and he kinda beat her up." I decided against sugarcoating anything and go all the way in.

"Kinda, huh?" The girl laughed, but didn't seem the least bit surprised.

"Yeah, and well, the way he was treating her concerned me. We're doing a story on the incident for *Rumor Central* and I was hoping we could get a statement from Mynique."

I decided to leave off the fact that I had video of the whole thing. I didn't know if she would run back and tell Mynique and then, it would get back to Tamara and Dexter, who would be ready to wring my neck if they found out I'd had this video all this time.

"Umph, she ain't gon' talk to you," the girl said and my heart sank. But then, she quickly said, "But I may. You want a story, huh?"

"Yes," I said a little too quickly.

"Well, I got a story for you," the girl continued, smacking her lips. "How much y'all pay?"

It was my turn to lose my excitement. "Well, we don't really pay for stories."

"Who pays then?" she asked. "Because what I know is worth some money."

"I don't really—"

"I heard the *National Enquirer* pays," she said, cutting me off.

I sighed. I'd lost quite a few stories from people who demanded to be paid in exchange for their dirt, but WXIA, the TV station I worked for, was adamant that we never give someone money in exchange for a story.

"Yes, the *Enquirer* pays, but we don't."

"Well, I need to be talking to them then." She paused, and for a minute I thought she was going to hang up. But finally she said, "You know what? Since I like you and you be rocking some bad outfits, I'm gonna give you a little somethin'-somethin'. This isn't the first time Demond done put them paws on her."

"Seriously?" I replied. I almost asked why she was selling her cousin out like that, but I'd been doing this long enough to know jealous family members and hating friends were usually the quickest ones to spill the dirt. Some, like this girl, spilled to the *National Enquirer* for money. Others talked for no other reason than they wanted to hurt the celebrity they were snitching on.

"So, you're telling me this isn't his first time beating her up?" I asked.

"You heard me. And not just her. Pretty boy had a history before he blew up as an actor. Do your homework. You'll see. I gotta go." She hesitated again, then said, "You don't have the number to the *National Enquirer*, do you?"

"Umm, no," I said even though I did. I wasn't about to help her sell her story to that tabloid.

"Fine, I'll call information." She hung up the phone before I could ask her any more questions.

She might not have given up the dirt directly, but she'd definitely piqued my interest and had me ready to go digging to find out more.

Chapter 9

I usually didn't answer calls from unknown numbers on my cell, but lately, I'd been missing quite a few scoops because of that. And the way Tamara was breathing down my neck about the lack of good gossip I was bringing in, I couldn't afford to miss anything. That's why I pushed the button to answer my cell right before the call went to voice mail.

"Hello, this May—"

"Trick, you've lost your mind!" The voice came bellowing through the phone before I could even get my name out good.

Even Tangie, my hairstylist, stopped curling my hair and frowned, that's how loud the caller was.

"Excuse me," I said. "Who is this?" I had thirty minutes before I went on air. I definitely didn't have time for any drama.

"I'm about to be your worst nightmare!" she screamed. That high-pitched nasally tone. The venom in her voice. Oh, there was no doubt who this was.

"Hi, Mynique," I casually said, holding up a finger to let Tangie know everything was fine. She still shook her head, but went back to work on my hair.

"Don't 'hi, Mynique' me, like we're friends or some-thing!" she snapped.

I tried to stay cool. "Girl, why are you dialing my phone, screaming at me like you've lost your mind?" I asked. I guess her cousin did know how to get in touch with her after all. "Shouldn't you be somewhere filing charges against your boyfriend?" I probably shouldn't have taken that jab, but oh, well.

She lowered her voice but her tone was still firm. "I told you, you need to mind your business. My cousin told me that you called there looking for me."

I wanted to ask her if her cousin also shared that she'd told me Demond had beat Mynique up before, but I decided to just let her rant.

"Why you calling my people?"

"I called the number that I found listed for you," I replied.

"Well, I don't live there."

"Okay, whatever. I found you now." To be honest, I didn't want to put the girl out there like that, which was why I hadn't told any of the producers about the video. I knew the minute Dexter saw it, he'd want to run it. And as much as I couldn't stand Mynique, I didn't want the world to see her getting beat like that. So, I was hoping she'd give me something, *any-thing* that would be enough to get Tamara off my back.

"You don't need to be looking for me at all," Mynique said. "I don't have anything to say to you."

"I called because I was trying to help you out." I didn't usually call people we were about to run a story on. We weren't the news, which needed to be objective and get the other side. So she needed to be thankful I was even trying to get her side.

"What part of 'I don't need your help' do you not get?" Mynique asked.

I pulled out one of the curls that Tangie had made too

tight. "Look, let's be real. We're not exactly friends," I said, leaning back in my chair.

"I wonder why? Let's see, number one, because you're a little girl and I'm a woman. Number two, you're a nosey, gossiping b—"

"My point is," I interrupted her, not bothering to tell her she may have been older but I was more woman than she would ever be, "regardless, if I see someone in an abusive relationship, then I'm gonna say something."

"You don't know anything about me!" Mynique said. It was strange. Her voice alternated between having an attitude and trembling, like she was scared but trying to act hard. "You're just jealous because I got a good man on my arm," she continued. "You and your nosey behind is gonna mess up the good thing I got going for me. I have all kinds of doors opening up for me now and I don't need you causing problems."

"Oh, is that why you're staying with him now, because you have doors opening up?" I asked. That didn't surprise me. That kind of thing happened all the time in the entertainment industry. But it surprised me that Mynique wanted fame that bad that she'd let herself get beat up.

"Don't you worry about why I'm staying with him. Worry about your own love life, or lack of a love life," she added. "Since rumor has it J. Love is back with his baby mama." I know she was trying to rile me up, and while that comment stung (I didn't even know if it was true or not), I refused to let her get to me.

"Yeah, I would rather be single than be with a guy who beats the crap out of me. Believe that," I replied. I needed to refocus, so I took a deep breath before I continued. "Anyway, I'm doing a story on *Rumor Central* on you and Demond, and I was just seeing if you wanted to make a statement, maybe give some advice to other women going through the same thing."

"Yeah, my advice is for everyone to get out of my business," Mynique said. "That's the advice I'm giving." Then, it actually sounded like her voice was cracking. "Why are you doing a freaking story on me anyway?"

"I thought you liked publicity. Didn't you come over to me at the club and give me the scoop on you and your boo so I could talk about you on my show? Well, I'm about to be talking about you on my show."

"Maya, don't play with me. I'm sick of you and your self-righteous attitude!" she screamed again, before lowering her voice. "What you fail to understand is that everybody can't fall back on Daddy's money. Some of us have to make it the best way we can."

"So, that is really what this is all about? You're letting this dude put his hands on you because you think he can help your career?"

She inhaled sharply. "Like I said, you don't need to worry about what I do or why I do it. Ya feel me?" She was back to tough-girl mode now.

Tangie swung me around to face the mirror so I could survey my hair. I leaned into the mirror and fluffed a few curls. "So, I guess that means that you won't be making a statement."

"No, I won't. And you listen to me and listen to me closely. Keep my name out of your mouth. Period. End of discussion."

"So it doesn't matter to you what kind of example you're setting?" I nodded to Tangie to let her know I liked my hair.

"I don't care about an example. I'm trying to do me and get paid in the process," Mynique replied.

"Wow" was all I could say.

"You all right?" Tangie mouthed as she started gathering up her supplies.

I nodded, rolling my eyes.

"I'm telling you now, if you put my name in your mouth, say anything about me on your show, you're going to regret it," Mynique threatened. "I promise you that. You don't want me as an enemy."

"Girl, bye." Maybe if Mynique had come to me in a different way, I might have cut her some slack. But she was definitely about to make sure she was put on extreme blast on my show. "The last thing you'll ever do is threaten me," I told her.

"You really want to take it there?" Mynique said.

"It's taken. Good luck with getting your butt beat" was all I said as I slammed the phone down.

I picked up the office phone and punched in the extension to Dexter's office. I glanced at the clock as the phone rang. Yep, I had enough time.

"What's up, Maya?"

"Change of plans, Dexter," I said, scrolling through my phone. "We still have about twenty minutes. I want to change the lead story."

"What? Change it? We air in twenty minutes!"

"Trust, you'll want this. I'm sending you some video that's going to make your day."

I found what I was looking for and pressed SEND.

Chapter 10

I probably should've felt guilty, but I didn't. Any piece of guilt I felt had gone out the window when Mynique Foxx snapped on me when all I was trying to do was help. No, if she wouldn't take my help that way, I was about to help her another way—by letting her see what a fool she looked like getting beat up by somebody who claimed to be her man.

"Stand by, Maya. We're up in five, four, three . . ." My director, Manny, gave me the cue to begin.

I let the theme music come up and then taper off before I began talking. "What's up, everybody? It's your girl, Maya Morgan, the fantabulous host of *Rumor Central*, where we dish the dirt on the celebrities you love. Boy, have we got some goodies for you today. The Rumor Mill is on fire." I turned to camera two, which I loved best because it had the best lighting. "Which D-list actress recently got publicly beat by her A-list boyfriend?" I paused for effect. "How about I can show you better than I can tell you?" I waited as the video came up. I could only shake my head as I once again watched Demond hit Mynique in the jaw like she was some dude off the street, then snatch her up by the hair and slam her against the wall.

"No, your eyes are not deceiving you," I continued. "That is hot, young actor Demond Cash. Yes, *that* Demond Cash. The star of the new John Singleton sequel *Boyz Back In The Hood*, and he is definitely acting like he's from the hood," I said. I fingered my platinum Tiffany necklace as I continued. "Word is that he's playing a thug in the upcoming flick and I guess he's getting his practice off screen as well, and his girlfriend, Mynique, is his punching bag. Don't recognize Mynique?" I laughed. "If you blinked, you missed her. She was a nineties sit-com star who had been looking to revitalize her career. Well, Mynique, girl, this ain't the way to do it," I said, giving my full Wendy Williams flavor. "But a little birdie told me this isn't Mynique and Demond's first public feud. In fact, we hear he makes no secret about how much he puts them paws on women. Of course, *Rumor Central* is staying all over this story and will keep you updated as we get more info. When we know it, you'll know it, too." I turned back to camera one. "More Bow Wow baby-mama drama. We'll have that story after the break."

The music came up again as I tossed to the commercial break. I knew Demond was going to be pissed, but he'd lost all major cool points with me when he'd put his hands on Mynique, so I couldn't care less about him being mad. And the way she had just acted with me, I definitely didn't care if she was mad.

"Hey, good stuff, Maya," Tamara called out, giving me the thumbs-up as she scurried across the studio. I used to really respect Tamara back when I worked for *Miami Divas*. Back then, she'd seemed like a serious journalist. Now, all she was was a Mona from *Love and Hip Hop* wannabe, constantly try-ing to chase her reality star, at anyone's expense. She had been getting on my nerves lately, but I was glad to expose Demond and his abusive ways.

Manny gave me the stand-by cue again and then, I came back and wrapped up the rest of the show, including my own personal two cents on why women shouldn't endure abuse. I closed with how women should love themselves enough to walk away and I gave the 800 domestic abuse hotline. I could only imagine Mynique sitting at home, fuming. She hated me with a passion as it was, so it's not like I had anything to lose, as if I cared about her anyway.

"Maya, absolutely loved it," Dexter said, catching up with me as I left the set. "That's the Maya we all know and love."

"Glad you liked it."

"Yep, some of your best work. But um, kill the commentary," he added.

I stopped and turned to face him. "Excuse me?"

"I'm just saying, we just want you to give us the dirt. Straight, no chaser."

I had no idea what in the world that meant, but it didn't sound good.

"I'm sorry. I don't understand."

He kept that stupid smile. "I'm saying, we love the dirt. Save the lectures for the other shows. All that 'love yourself' crap. Nobody wants to hear it."

"Maybe some people *need* to hear it," I replied.

Ugh, Dexter made me sick. Was it so bad that I wanted to be more than just some sleazy gossip show? But Dexter was ten times worse than Tamara, so arguing with him would be pointless.

"Fine, Dexter," I said, turning and continuing down the hallway. It wasn't like I had plans to be lecturing anybody, but if I felt like adding my two cents on a story, I should be able to.

I had just made it back into my office when my telephone rang. A few months ago, I'd had a stalker and then my fan base had gotten ridiculous, so I had made it a point to have all of my phone calls screened. That's why I was surprised when Sheryl, the front receptionist came on and said, "Hey, Maya, there's a girl on the phone and she really wants to talk to you." I raised an eyebrow. Sheryl knew I didn't take random calls. She must've sensed my hesitation because she added, "She's crying and I don't know, but my gut tells me you should speak to her."

I let out a heavy sigh. I was tired but decided to see what Sheryl was talking about.

"Hello," I said, picking up the phone.

"Hi, Maya Morgan?" the voice softly said.

"Hi, this is she. How may I help you?"

"Um, you don't know me but I just . . ." The girl hesitated and sniffed like she had seriously been crying. "I just wanted to say thank you."

"You're welcome, but thank you for what?" I asked, dropping down in my chair and removing my Chanel pumps.

"I think you may have just saved my life."

Now that made me sit up. I'd gotten lots of calls since I had been doing *Rumor Central*, but never one claiming that I had saved someone's life.

"What do you mean?" I said, giving her my undivided attention now.

"Well, my boyfriend . . . I—I just . . ." She was stammering and I wanted to tell her to spit it out because I needed to go home.

"My boyfriend," she finally continued. "He's really abusive and it wasn't until . . ." She inhaled sharply like it was taking all of her strength just to talk to me. "I really respect you a lot and it wasn't until seeing you on TV and how you told women to have more respect for themselves and seeing what Demond did to Mynique, that I saw myself. You're right, I deserve better. I had been all ready to give him a second chance and then I saw your show, and well, I'm not going to do it no matter how much he begs. And I just wanted to thank you for that. That's all I wanted."

Wow, I wanted to say. When I'd given my little spiel, I'd never had any idea it would actually reach someone. The power of TV.

"Thank you so much," I said. "What's your na—" She hung up before I could finish my sentence. I was a little shocked because I'd never even remotely considered that my story, which I had just intended to be gossip, would help someone else. Even when I'd told Dexter that maybe someone needed to hear what I had to say, I hadn't actually believed it. I leaned back in my chair and smiled. I hadn't considered it, but I was definitely glad that it had.

Chapter 11

Dinner with my parents sucks. That's all I could think as I sat here, toying with my cedar planked salmon as my mother gushed about yet another shopping trip. This time she was heading to Paris. My mother needed to be inducted into the shopping hall of fame. My dad kept trying to rein in her spending, but it never seemed to work. I think now he just told himself that was something he'd have to deal with.

This dinner was his idea. He'd been complaining that we didn't spend enough family time together. But I was seventeen, going on eighteen. It was too late to play *Brady Bunch* family now. Since I was still trying to stay on my dad's good side so he'd keep paying my American Express bill, I kept my mouth closed.

"So, Maya, how's the show going?" he asked.

My dad had seen one, maybe two episodes. He said he couldn't take all the frivolous gossip. My mom watched, but sometimes, I felt like it was only to critique and make sure I was representing Liza Morgan well.

"It's going fine," I said. "I'm still on top."

My dad took a bite of his asparagus. "And I would expect nothing less. Nobody can hold a candle to Maya Morgan."

That's why I would always be a daddy's girl, because he knew just what to say.

When we first sat down for dinner, I suddenly found myself wishing that Travis were here. But since he'd found out about Aunt Bev, he hadn't wanted to do much of anything. He just went to school and came home. He'd even left the girls alone, and believe me, they were not happy.

"So, are you ready for graduation?" my dad asked after a few more minutes. "Have you decided on a college?"

I would never tell my father, but I wanted to ditch college altogether. People went to college to get a good job, and make a lot of money. Well, I had a good job that paid a lot of money so I didn't see the purpose of college. But of course, my dad wasn't hearing that at all so I just said, "I'm waiting on my acceptance letter to the University of Miami."

My father patted my hand. "Well, I have no doubt you'll get in. I'm really proud of you, Maya," he said.

I glanced at my watch to try and see how much longer I was going to have to endure this dinner. My parents were cool, but who wanted to hang with their parents on a Saturday night?

My phone rang and my father gave a disapproving look. I knew he wanted my phone off during dinner, but he didn't turn his off and I was just as important.

"I have to go to the restroom," I said, standing and grabbing my phone.

"Maya!" my father said.

"Oh, honey, relax." My mother patted his hand. He called her his stress diffuser because outside of shopping, she had the awesome ability to calm him down. It worked once again, and that gave me the opportunity to escape.

"Be right back," I said, scurrying off.

"Hey, Alvin." I answered the phone right before it went to voice mail.

"Hey, beautiful," he replied.

"What are you doing?"

"Nothing, just wanted to see if you wanted to go catch a movie."

"I'm at dinner with the folks," I told him.

"Oh yeah, I forgot your once-a-month Saturday dinner."

"And I'm counting down until it's time to go. They are driving me crazy." Honestly, they hadn't really done anything other than ask a bunch of questions, but still, who wanted to do that?

"Well, I think it's cool that your dad insists that you guys have this dinner," Alvin said.

"Yeah, whatever. What are you doing?" I leaned in the mirror to check and make sure my hair and makeup was on point.

"I was just chillin' and thought of you."

That made me smile. "Where's your girlfriend, Pine-Sol?" I asked.

He laughed. "I keep telling you, *Marisol* is not my girlfriend. She's just a close friend."

"Umph."

Marisol—yes, I knew her name—had been hanging out with Alvin for the past few months. A pretty, olive-skinned Jennifer Lopez lookalike, she seemed to be really feeling Alvin. Personally, I think she was feeling Alvin's money, because he had a lot of it. But I did think Alvin liked her a lot more than he let on.

"I told you, all you have to do is say you'll be mine and you don't ever have to worry about me talking to her again," Alvin said. I could feel his smile through the phone.

I couldn't help but smile, too, as I exited the bathroom. But that smile quickly faded when I saw the couple standing up to exit a booth in the back of the restaurant. They leaned in and kissed like they were in the middle of some stupid romance movie.

"Oh, my God," I mumbled.

"What?" Alvin said. "Maya, what's wrong?" he repeated when I didn't answer.

"I just saw Sheridan's boyfriend."

"Who?"

"Sheridan Matthews, my BFF. Her boyfriend, Javier, is here with another girl."

I moved closer to their table. First, Kennedi's boyfriend was cheating, now Sheridan's?

"Un-unh. I don't think so," I hissed as they got out of the booth. He took the girl's hand to lead her away. "They're leaving. Let me call you back," I quickly said.

"Maya, what are you about to do?" Alvin said.

"Let me call you back," I repeated. I hung up and raced to catch up with them just as they reached the door.

"Javier," I called out to him. He ignored me as he quickly pushed his date out the door.

"No, he didn't," I mumbled. I raced outside, trying to pull up my camera app at the same time. I was going to post pictures of his cheating behind on Instagram.

Just as I opened up the camera app, I noticed my battery was at one percent. "Come on, don't die," I muttered as I held the camera up. He looked at me in shock, but it gave me the perfect angle and I managed to snap one good time, as he backed away and sped out of the parking lot.

Chapter 12

I couldn't get out of that dinner with my parents fast enough. When I got back to the table, I gulped down my food. I wanted to leave and go find someplace to charge my phone, but I knew my dad would have a stroke. When I got back to the table, he was already giving me the side eye.

"Can I use your phone real quick?" I asked him.

"Maya," my mom said. "This is our time."

"No, it's an emergency." I needed to call Sheridan right away.

"No, you may not use my phone," my father said, sliding his BlackBerry closer to him. "This is family time."

I cut my eyes. "Then why is *your* phone out?"

"Maya Camille Simone Morgan, don't get sassy," my mother said, using my full name, which she did whenever I was pushing her buttons.

I slunk back in my seat. "I'm sorry. It's just that it's an emergency."

"Is someone dying?" my father asked.

"No, but—"

"Well, then there's no emergency. The only people that matter right now is our family," he said, matter-of-factly.

"Well, why does Travis not have to be here?" I asked.

"You know why, Maya," my mother said, her tone chastising. "Don't act like that."

My father took a deep breath. "But I guess now's a good a time as any to tell you, we're going to send Travis back to Brooklyn."

"What?" I exclaimed.

A sad expression crept up on my dad's face. "My sister is pretty sick, and although she doesn't want Travis there, it's killing him."

I definitely agreed with that. It almost felt like my cousin was sinking into a depression.

"And we think if something happened to Bev and he wasn't there, he'd never forgive himself," my mom added.

"So, you think something is going to happen to her?" I asked. "I thought she was out of danger? Is she going to die?"

"We hope not, but truthfully, it's not looking good," my dad admitted.

I had no more words. I was sad for Aunt Bev, and also for Travis. And I was definitely going to miss him, because we'd had a great time even though he'd only been here a few months.

"I'll be going up there next week myself," my dad added. "Hopefully, Beverly will respond to this latest round of chemo."

My mother smiled. "But we're going to think positive, send positive vibes up to New York."

I nodded, but didn't say anything else as I went back to fumbling with my food.

My parents made some more small talk and I was so grateful when my father finally called for the bill. He paid it and we made our way back to his Bentley. As soon as we got into the car I plugged my phone in. I was wishing that I had one of those super-fast chargers but we were almost home by the time the little Apple sign finally came back on my phone.

I immediately punched in Sheridan's number the minute I got enough bars on my phone.

"Hey, where are you?"

"I'm at home. Why?"

"I'm on my way over there." I knew this was something I needed to tell Sheridan face-to-face. I would've texted her the picture, but I needed to show her in person. So, I didn't even go in the house. I just told my parents I'd be right back and jumped in my car. It took me fifteen minutes to get to Sheridan's house. I punched in the buttons on her security system and she immediately buzzed me in.

"Where's the fire?" she said, after I had parked and raced inside her mansion.

"No, the question you should be asking yourself is 'where's your boyfriend?' "

"Huh?" she said, looking confused. "He's at home sick."

"Oh, is that what he told you?" I stopped in her foyer and turned to face her.

"Um"—she held up her phone—"I'm on the phone with him now." She pushed the button and put him on speakerphone. "Javier?"

I heard a cough. *Really, dude?*

"Yeah, babe. What's up?"

"Um, Maya just got here," Sheridan said.

"Okay. Go hang out with your friend. I'm going to go lay back down. This flu is kicking my butt." His voice was all husky like he was straining to talk.

"Get better soon, baby," she said, smiling. "You want me to bring you something?"

"Nah," he said, his voice sounding all weak. "My mom is here. She's supposed to be making me some soup or something."

Was this dude for real? That's all I could think as I stood there watching the phone with my mouth on the floor.

"All right, baby. Call me if you need anything."

Sheridan hung the phone up and I looked at my friend in disbelief.

"He is straight playing you," I said.

"What are you talking about, Maya?" Sheridan walked into her living room. "I just don't get your obsession with him."

"I'm not obsessed with your man."

"That's what he calls it," she said.

I threw up my hands. "Oh, give me a freakin' break. I'm not obsessed with your man. I don't like him because he's disrespectful and abusive."

"No, he is not," she said, defending him.

I dug in my purse and pulled out my phone. "He's also a cheat."

"What are you talking about, Maya?" She opened the refrigerator, pulled out a bottled water, opened it, and took a sip.

"I just saw Javier at dinner," I said. "With another girl."

She spun around to face me. "No, you didn't. He's at home sick."

"No, he wants you to *believe* he's at home, but he just left Sullivan Steakhouse with another chick."

"Maya, here we go again," she huffed as she folded her arms, not taking the phone. "Is there any guy you like me with?"

"How 'bout you find one that's faithful," I said.

"I really wish you'd stay out of my business," Sheridan said.

We'd almost lost our friendship when she got with Travis against my advice, so fine. I was just going to leave it alone. If she wanted to be played by a guy *again,* then I was going to let her.

"Fine, Sheridan," I said. "Since it's obvious you believe your *new* boyfriend over your *old* BFF."

"Maya, don't even be like that," she said, cutting me off. "I didn't say that I believe one over the other. I'm just saying you're mistaken. I've been on the phone with Javier for the last twenty minutes and he's sick. He was sick earlier today."

"You just believe anything, don't you? He *lied* earlier today just like he was lying now."

"You're being such a drama queen," she said. "All I'm saying is that you're mistaken. You saw somebody else. Not him."

I thrust my phone at her. "I'm not crazy. Look. I snapped a picture of him."

She kept her eyes on me as she reluctantly took my phone. She looked at the picture, then back at me. "Just wow."

"Yeah, I know, right. Just wow. He's a dog."

"No, wow to you," Sheridan said. "You're a trip."

"What is that supposed to mean?" I asked.

She all but threw my phone back at me. "That's not Javier, smart aleck. That's his twin brother, Jose."

"What?" I said, stunned. "What do you mean twin? Javier has a twin?"

"Yes," Sheridan replied, and I could tell she was getting really mad. "They don't mess with him because he's nothing but trouble, but if you look closer, he has streaks in his hair. Javier doesn't."

I stared at the picture on my phone for a few minutes. He looked just like Javier! But there were streaks in his hair, and now that I was looking closer, I saw this guy was a little stockier than Javier. Oh, no. What had I done?

"Sheridan, I . . . I—"

She held up her hand. "Save it," she replied. "You are trippin' for real and I don't get why. But I'm real sick and tired of it." She headed to her front door, then swung it open. "And I'm sick and tired of you, so please exit to the left." She motioned out her front door.

I didn't know what to say or do, so I did the only thing I could. I walked out.

Chapter 13

When Sheridan and I had agreed to put our lockers next to each other freshman year, I'd thought it was a really good idea. But this past year, I'd had more times than not that I regretted that decision.

Today was one of those times.

I just was not in the mood. She was going to mess around and say the wrong thing to me and I might snap. I took my time approaching my locker. Sheridan was digging for something inside of hers.

"So, you're not speaking?" I said, opening my locker up and tossing my binder inside.

"I was here first. Seems like you should be speaking to me," she said all nonchalantly.

I really didn't feel like fighting with her anymore. "Look, Sheridan," I said, deciding to take the high road. "I'm sorry if I made you mad about Javier. I'm just worried about you, that's all."

Sheridan shut her locker and glared at me. "I told you, you don't need to worry about me. I'm a big girl. I can handle myself."

"Whatever you say." I held my hands up in defense.

She stepped in my face. I couldn't tell if she was trying to jump bad or make her point. "You think I've liked every guy you've dated? I think Bryce is a snob, J. Love is an arrogant jerk, and you're sleeping on Alvin. But I didn't try and tell you what you should and shouldn't do with them. I minded my business and let you love who you wanted to love. And I don't understand why it's so hard for you to give me that same respect."

Wow. I had no idea that she felt that way. "As a friend, you should've told me if you didn't like my boyfriends."

"No, as a friend, I let you do you. No, they weren't my cup of tea—including Bryce, because you know that whole mess with him was because I was mad. But they weren't for me to like. If you liked them, I loved them."

I stood speechless for a minute, before finally throwing my hands up and saying, "Okay, fine."

"Fine. Hopefully we don't have this discussion anymore. I gotta get to class." She spun around and bumped right into Shay, Bali, and Evian. They traveled like a pack of wolves now.

"What's up, Sheridan?" Bali said.

"Hey, girl," Evian added.

"Did you get your invitation to Bali's birthday bash?" Shay asked.

I couldn't make out what Sheridan said, but she was smiling, which I guess meant that she had.

Then, they completely ignored me as they brushed past me. I wondered if they really thought they were hurting my feelings by not speaking to me and not inviting me to a lame high school party. I partied with superstars. They could keep their little busted parties.

Evian actually stopped and ran back over to me. "Hey," she whispered, "you might want to go check on your girl."

"Check on who?" I asked. Evian hadn't said much to me

over the past few weeks. I really think she was ashamed because she'd sunk to an all-time low over spring break when
she'd faked her own kidnapping.

Both Shay and Bali side-eyed her, like they were mad that
she was talking to me. But she ignored them and continued
talking. "Kennedi. She's in the bathroom. She's crying and I
think she's hurt."

I took off toward the girls' bathroom. As soon as I opened
the door, I could see that it was empty. I looked under the
stalls and in the third one, saw Kennedi's UGG sneakers.

"Hey, K. You all right?" She didn't answer. "K," I repeated,
"it's Maya. Don't make me climb over the stall."

There was a pause, then the door clicked, and opened.
"You know you're not about to climb over a bathroom stall,"
she said, trying to force a smile.

"Well, you're right about that, but I needed to get you
out." I studied her. Her hair was disheveled and her eyes red,
like she'd been fighting and crying. "What's wrong with you?"

It was then that I noticed the bruise on her right cheek.
"OMG, what happened to you?"

"I fell," she said, brushing past me.

"You fell? Where?"

"On my way to school."

I couldn't help but stare at her. I knew that Kendrick had
dropped her off at school today because I'd seen her sitting in
his truck when we got to campus.

"How could you fall and get a bruise like that?" I demanded to know.

"I just did, okay! Leave it alone."

"Did Kendrick do this?" I asked, feeling my anger already
building. She didn't have to tell me the truth. I already knew.

"Maya, chill, okay?" She leaned in the mirror and examined her face. Then, she reached in her clutch and pulled out
some face powder and dabbed it over the bruise.

"Seriously?" I pointed at her face. "That's okay with you?"

"Maya, it's not even like that. Just stay out of it. You don't know nothing about nothing." She dropped the compact back in her purse. "You know what? I'm out. If Ms. Clark asks where I went, tell her I'm sick."

Kennedi stormed out of the bathroom. I debated following her, but I knew it wouldn't do any good. This was the last straw. I made a mental note that I was going to do some digging. I needed to get through to my friends. Maybe some hard statistics would do it. I doubted it, but I needed to at least try.

Chapter 14

I would never understand why a girl thought it was okay to let her guy put his hands on her. But obviously, there were a lot of girls who didn't feel the same way. That was all I could think as I read all the stories of domestic abuse.

I'd sat down at my desk to do some research, thinking I'd pull up a few stories here or there. But the number of young people dealing with domestic abuse was mind blowing. I'd thought that only people with low self-esteem and no love for themselves would put themselves in a situation where they'd be beat up by someone that was supposed to care about them. But as I read story after story, I knew that wasn't the case at all. These were stories from honor roll students, from girls who were rich, poor, black, white, from all religions. Each of them enduring pain in the name of love.

I'd loved my ex, Bryce, something crazy. But I'd loved *me* more. That's why we weren't together now. He hadn't treated me like the queen that I was, so he'd had to go. I was having a hard time understanding the mindset that allowed a person to be in an abusive relationship, and the whole "he hit me because he loves me" mentality made no sense to me. Love didn't hurt. Period.

I sadly shook my head as I clicked PRINT on yet another article about Demond Cash's abusive history. Apparently, he'd been arrested for domestic assault three years ago. But it was before he'd become a big-time actor so it wasn't well known.

Mynique needed to be thanking me for exposing her man for the creep that he was because anyone who would throw her around like Demond did needed to be put on blast. And even though she couldn't see it now, I had no doubt that one day she would.

I looked up from my desk to see security racing down the hallway. I stood up and poked my head out my office door.

"What's going on?" I asked Shelby, one of the production assistants.

"You," she said, a worried look across her face.

"What does that mean?" I asked.

"You over here creating drama, girl." She pointed toward the front lobby. "Apparently, the people at the front are demanding to see you."

"Me? Who is it? And what did I do? I'm in my office minding my business."

"Demond Cash and Mynique Foxx," she said like that was the worst thing ever.

I hadn't heard from Demond since my story aired. I knew he wasn't happy about it because Mynique had called and cussed me out all kinds of ways. Or rather, cussed my voice mail out because I never answered her countless phone calls.

"He wants to talk to you," Shelby said.

Oh, no way. I wasn't about to go up there and talk to Demond face to face. I wasn't a scaredy cat and I stood by everything I said, but I wasn't crazy either.

I don't know if Shelby read the look on my face, but she said, "Don't worry about it. It looks like security has it handled."

I was about to turn and go back to my office and lock the

door when Tamara came racing down the hall. She stopped and looked at me. Worry lines creased her brow.

"Was everything legit?" she said.

"Of course," I replied.

She didn't say another word as she pushed the glass door open that led out into the lobby.

I immediately heard Demond going in. "Where is she? I want to talk to her! I demand a retraction. You people can't just air anything you feel like whenever . . ." His voice trailed off as the lobby door closed.

I debated going back into my office, but I really wanted to know what he was saying. So, I moved closer to the lobby so I could try and hear the conversation. I needed to know everything that was said in case they tried to lie on me and get me in trouble.

"Sir, calm down," Reggie, the security guard, told him. "Now, we're going to have to ask you once again to exit the premises."

"I'm not going anywhere until I talk to Maya!" he demanded.

I heard Tamara say something, but I couldn't make it out, so I eased a little closer, and just my luck, my stiletto got caught in the carpet and I went tumbling to the ground.

All eyes turned in my direction. I eased up off the floor with as much grace as I could muster. Then, I had to make a split-second decision whether to run in the opposite direction or face Demond.

"Maya, I see you," Demond screamed. "If you woman enough to go on air talking all that garbage, you should be woman enough to face us."

I stood contemplating my next move. I decided that since security was there, there really was no reason for me to be scared, so I pushed the lobby door open.

I raised an eyebrow in a "what?" gesture and waited for him to say something. "May I help you?" I finally said.

"How dare you air that story?" Demond yelled at me. "We demand that you do an interview with both of us"—he pointed between him and Mynique—"so that she can tell you that we were just playing around."

Mynique stood looking like some kind of dumb puppet, which was shocking because she always acted big and bad with me.

"If you don't do our interview, I'm gonna own this friggin' TV station," Demond snapped.

"You forget that I was there," I told him. "I saw the way you smacked Mynique." Mynique cringed when I said that, but still she said nothing. "I know you weren't playing around."

"You little . . ." Demond lunged toward me, but luckily, Reggie grabbed him from behind in a big bear hug.

"You itching to go to jail today, huh?" Reggie said.

Demond squirmed to try and break free, but Reggie had a tight grip on him.

"You don't need any more bad press, Demond," Tamara said, "so, I suggest you do like Reggie said and leave, because the cops should be here any minute now."

Demond glared at me for a minute. If he could've strangled me to death right then, I have no doubt he would have. Luckily, Reggie gripped his arm a little harder just in case he was getting any ideas. Demond snatched his body away from Reggie. "If I were you, I'd watch my back," he told me. Then he stomped toward the door. "Come on, Mynique."

Mynique looked at me and for once, I didn't see arrogance. I didn't see hate. I simply saw fear, and I knew this thing with Mynique and Demond ran a lot deeper than any of us knew.

Chapter 15

I needed to put all the boy trouble of my friends (and enemies like Mynique) aside. That fear in Mynique's eyes had been haunting me, and the drama with Sheridan and Kennedi made me mad. But standing here looking at my cousin, Travis, with his suitcases on the floor next to him—that made me sad.

And sad trumped mad any day.

When Travis had shown up at my house and my dad had announced that Travis would be staying with us, I had not been happy. I was an only child, used to being an only child, and I hadn't been trying to share my parents with anyone. But Travis had come in and done what he always did, made me laugh and proved why he was my favorite cousin. Yeah, he'd almost gotten me in some major trouble by hooking me up with his drug-dealing friend a few months ago. But Travis had been ready to take full responsibility. And we'd gotten caught up in some major drama. Besides the fact that trouble seemed to always follow him, Travis really was a good guy. A playa when it came to the girls—but still a good guy. Hence, the reason why he was giving up his senior year at a school where he had quickly fit in to go home and be with his sick mother.

"How's Aunt Bev?" I asked him.

Travis shrugged, and I could tell he was trying to be strong. "They said she may . . . she may . . ." He couldn't even get the words out. But I'd heard my mom and dad talking earlier. They thought Aunt Bev only had a few weeks to live. The breast cancer was back and more aggressive than ever. The pneumonia had made her immune system weak, and apparently, she was in her final days.

"Come on, son," my dad said, stepping up on the side of Travis. He patted Travis's back. "It doesn't matter what the doctor says. We know there's a higher power that has the final say."

Travis nodded, even though I could tell he didn't really believe it. I wasn't some religious freak, but I was definitely going to send up a prayer for Aunt Bev tonight. I would pray for Travis, too. He'd already lost a brother to gang violence. I don't know what he would do if he lost his mother, too.

"All right, son. We'd better get going," my dad said, reaching down and picking up his luggage. "We need to make sure we don't miss that flight."

I looked at Travis and had to struggle not to cry myself. I'd never even realized until that very moment how much weight my cousin bore on his shoulders. "Stay strong, okay?"

"Yeah, I'm good." He managed a smile. "You know how I do it."

I wanted to end on a happy note, so I added, "And don't be picking up any girls at the hospital."

He playfully hit my shoulder. "I don't pick up girls. Girls pick up me."

I was happy that he was trying to remain upbeat. He hugged me good-bye, squeezing me just a little bit tighter than normal. Then, he hugged my teary-eyed mom, before he and my dad walked out the door.

As I watched them walk away, I wondered how I would feel if I ever lost one of my parents. The thought tore at my insides. As lame as they could be, I still loved my parents.

Scratch being sad, I'd rather go back to being mad.

I made my way back upstairs, debating whether I should borrow our maid, Sui's phone and call Kennedi since I had the feeling she was ignoring my calls, as they kept going straight to voice mail. But before I could make a decision, my cell phone rang and J. Love's picture popped up.

"House of beauty, this is cutie," I said, even though I wasn't my usual chipper self. But I thought maybe if I tried to be up-beat, my attitude would improve.

"Oh, I must have the wrong number," J. replied. "Because the girl I'm calling is gorgeous. Stunning. Ain't nothing *cute* about her."

I plopped down across my bed. "You always know the right things to say."

"Then why can't I get you to be my girl?"

" 'Cause you had me as your girl and you didn't know what to do with me," I replied as I curled a strand of hair around my finger.

"True dat," he said. "But I know now, and like my grandma says, when you know better, you do better."

"Boy, what do you want?" I said. I could just imagine him sitting up in some fancy hotel, his Timbs propped up on the coffee table, rocking his saggy jeans and colorful Elevate shirt. He was a spokesperson for that hip-hop clothing company so he didn't go anywhere without their gear on.

"I was just calling to see if I could fly you up to Vegas for my concert next week," J. Love said.

"Oh, yeah, let me go tell my mom I'm gonna go spend the weekend in Vegas with my ex-boyfriend," I sarcastically replied.

"Dang, I keep forgetting your mom got that leash on you," he chuckled.

"Yeah, everybody ain't got it like you and can be emanci-pated at fifteen."

"Shoot, my parents just trying to get paid." Though he laughed, I could hear the pain in his voice. When J. Love had released his first hit record, he'd made the news because his parents had spent every dime of his money on lavish cars and houses. He'd had to file bankruptcy at fifteen. He got emancipated right after that and a year later, he was pushing out another hit record and landing back on top.

"Well, me coming to meet you in Vegas is not an option," I told him.

"You got another man? Is that why you can't come?"

"Boy, I can't come because my mom would kill me and my dad would kill you. And it's not like I could lie with the way that the paparazzi stalks us. And why is that any of your business if I did have a man?" I added.

"Because I know it's only so long a fine thing like you is going to be single."

"Honey, you boys are nothing but trouble."

"That's why you need to get you a man."

I imagined him stroking his small goatee, with that cute, cocky smile, and just shook my head. "Whatever, J."

"You and nerd boy kicking it?" he asked.

"You can talk about Alvin all you want, but his bank account speaks for itself."

"Yeah, I know. His pockets are pretty fat."

That made me sit up. "How do you know anything about him?"

"Oh, you'd better believe I had ol' boy checked out. I had to know my competition."

I just laughed. "Okay, J. Love."

"On the real, you been doing okay?" he asked.

"I just had to say good-bye to my cousin. He's moving back home." I closed my eyes, inhaled, then exhaled, trying to fight off any tears. "Then, I'm going through some drama with my friends."

"Oh," was all he said. I knew J. Love had no interest in anything other than us, so I asked, "Have you heard from Mynique?"

"I told you I don't mess with her like that," he answered. "Besides, she ain't nothing but trouble. The way she flirts with dudes is gon' get her hurt."

"You should know," I said.

"Hey, I didn't flirt with her. And I'm just saying. Dudes don't like being disrespected like that and your girl is a trip."

"She ain't my girl," I said. "But whatever. If she wants to get beat up, more power to her. Not my problem."

As soon as the words left my mouth, I wondered if I'd one day be saying the same thing about my two best friends.

Chapter 16

This girl is really ignoring me! I pressed END on my phone and tossed it onto the table. I hadn't heard from Sheridan in two days and as friends who talked to each other every day, that was completely out of the ordinary. The only time we'd gone this long without talking was back when we had all that *Miami Divas* drama. I know she couldn't still be mad about me mistaking Jose for Javier. I'd apologized. Good grief, what else did she want?

Sheridan hadn't been at school yesterday and today she hadn't been answering my calls. I was about to get an attitude in a minute.

"Do you think she's still mad at me about Javier?" I asked Kennedi, who was sitting there staring out the window of my second-floor bedroom. Her being mad at me hadn't lasted long. She'd come up to me at school, acting like she hadn't been ignoring me, then said that she was coming home with me.

"I don't know," Kennedi said. I so could not appreciate her nonchalant attitude when I had some real issues that I was dealing with.

"Do you think I should dye my hair pink and join a rock band?" I asked her.

"I don't know," Kennedi said as she continued staring out the window.

"Hey, what is wrong with you?"

Since we'd walked into my room more than an hour ago, Kennedi hadn't said more than a few words. She kept looking at her phone and pacing back and forth. I'd asked her over a dozen times what was wrong. She'd said nothing, but it was obvious something was bothering my friend. She swore it wasn't Kendrick, but I didn't see how it could be anything else.

I had gone and picked her up because she was so down. She'd wrecked her car (her third wreck), so her dad wouldn't let her drive. If it wasn't the car and it wasn't Kendrick, I don't know what it was.

"I keep telling you nothing. I wish you would quit nagging me. You worse than my mama," she said, snapping.

She made me stop in my tracks. I just stared at her and she gave me this look like she was really irritated with me.

"Just because I'm not concerned with your little trivial drama about your fake friend, don't start tripping with me," she continued.

It took a moment for me to compose myself, but finally, I said, "Whoa, someone needs to take a chill pill. What the heck is your problem?"

I knew that Sheridan and Kennedi really didn't cut for each other, but over the past year they'd learned to get along so I didn't know what all of this was about.

Before I could say another word, Kennedi's phone rang. She must've broken her neck darting across the room to get her phone, which was sitting on the dresser.

"Hello?" she answered. I saw her let out a frustrated sigh. "I'm all right, Mom . . . No . . . What number is this you're calling me from? No, I'm cool. Nothing's wrong. I'll call you back later." She hung up the phone.

I raised an eyebrow. "Now, do you want to tell me what's going on? Because you're snapping at your mom like you're on one of those Disney Channel shows. You know Laura don't play that."

Kennedi plopped down on the edge of the bed. "It's Kendrick," she finally admitted.

Of course it is, I wanted to say.

"What did Kendrick do now?" I asked. *Besides bust you upside your head,* I wanted to add, but didn't.

"He's not returning my phone calls."

I sat down next to her. It was time we had a real heart-to-heart because her obsession with this dude was borderline scary. "Kennedi, what's really going on? You've never been into a guy like this where you're getting all worked up and upset."

"I told you, Kendrick is different. We were meant to be together and now he's talking about he thinks we need some space," she spat, as she got up and started walking back and forth across the room. "Unh-unh, see he's not about to play me like that. I gave him all of me—"

I jumped up. "Whoa, Hold on, wait a minute. What do you mean, you gave him all of you?"

"What do you *think* it means?" she snapped.

I didn't know whether to be hurt or shocked. Kennedi was the "I'm waiting till I get married" queen, so the fact that she'd chosen to lose her virginity to Kendrick was a shock within itself. But the fact that she hadn't told me about it cut me to the core.

"Wow, I cannot believe that," I said.

"Can't believe what?"

"That you didn't tell me that," I said, stunned.

"I was going to," she snapped. She ran her fingers through her long curly hair like she was really agitated. "You just don't understand. I have a lot going on."

I stood to face her. I wanted to look her right in the eye because this had really hurt my feelings.

"You're right. I don't understand at all. I thought you and I were BFFs."

She rolled her eyes. "Whatever, Maya. You've got a new BFF."

"So is that why you didn't tell me? Because I'm friends with Sheridan?"

She let out a heavy sigh again. "Look, Maya, I'm seriously stressed out. I don't want to fight with you. I didn't tell you because I didn't want to hear your mouth."

"Hear my mouth? What does that mean?"

"You can be so judgmental sometimes. Like now." She pushed past me and headed to the other side of the room.

I turned around, too. "No, I'm just not understanding why it is my friend is all of a sudden acting like some kind of a mad woman behind this dude."

She spun around and I could see that she was crying. "He's not just any dude. He's my first, and as far as I'm concerned, my last."

"And what is that supposed to mean?"

"Just"—she looked around—"can you just drive me to his house?"

"Kennedi," I said, "I'm not about to go stalking some guy."

"You're not *stalking* him. I'm just trying to find him."

"And if he wanted to be found he'd answer your phone calls," I said because I knew she had called him a hundred times.

She fell down on the bed and burst into tears. "What am I going to do? What in the world am I going to do?"

I know I probably should've walked over, hugged her, and comforted her or something, but I was too busy trying to figure out who in the world was this person lying on my bed and what in the world had she done with my friend.

Chapter 17

I could not believe I was doing this, driving around like some hood rat chick, trying to track down a man.

My BFF had clearly lost her mind.

"Turn right there," she hurriedly said.

I side-eyed her, but turned in the direction she was pointing. I had initially refused to drive her so she'd asked to use my ride. She was all teary eyed and worked up, and the way she was on edge, she definitely didn't need to be behind the wheel of a car, especially my car, so here I was driving around town like I was a human LoJack.

The first place we'd gone had been a bust. I'd almost died from embarrassment when Kendrick's mom had looked at Kennedi like she was some kind of crazed stalker and said, "Honey, why are you over here trying to track down my son?"

Kennedi hadn't even answered the woman; she'd just turned and stomped back toward the car. I could tell by the look on the woman's face, she was not a fan of Kennedi's.

Kennedi put another address in her phone's GPS and then thrust it toward me. "Here, follow the directions."

Watching her at Kendrick's house was strange enough,

but now, watching the way she was rocking back and forth, wringing her hands, I was convinced—my friend had flipped.

We drove in silence for about ten minutes, and then she said, "Right here," as she pointed to the right.

"Where are we?" I asked, as I slowed down in front of the small wooden home.

"This is his friend Lucas's house." She leaned up and looked up and down the row of cars parked along the street. "I bet he's over here."

The sun was setting and this wasn't an area I wanted darkness to catch me in. I was just about to say something when she sat up.

"See! There's his truck," she said, pointing down near the corner. "I knew he was over here!"

"Kennedi, what is going on with you?"

"Maya, don't start with me, okay?"

I was speechless as I shook my head and pulled over to the curb. Kennedi barely gave the car time to stop before she jumped out. Everything inside me told me to stay my behind in the car so I wouldn't have to witness my girl acting a fool, so I sat there twiddling my thumbs against the steering wheel. I sat there five, then ten minutes, but then I got worried as I heard screaming and yelling. I jumped out of the car and raced up the walkway. I had barely made it to the door when it swung open and Kennedi came out, her hair out of the loose ponytail that she'd had when she'd gone in.

"Oh, my God! Kennedi, what happened?" I asked.

"Nothing," she said, crying as she tried to push past me. "Let's just go."

I grabbed her to stop her. "Are you okay?" She was sobbing but wouldn't turn around. I looked up toward the house. Kendrick was standing on the porch looking mad as all get out, balling his fist up as he was taking deep breaths. Several people had trickled out on the porch as well, including some girls.

Kendrick glared in our direction, his chest heaving.

"What did you do to her?" I screamed as I pulled her close to me. I was two seconds from calling the cops.

"You need to get your girl" was all he replied.

"You're up here with all these other chicks all over you," I spat. "You lying dog."

"No, boo-boo," one of the girls with long, blond braids said, "he's all over *us*."

"And you and your desperate friend need to get out of here before somebody gets hurt," said another girl—well, I guess she was a girl. She had a low-cut fade, a wife beater, baggy jeans, and Timberlands.

The other girls all looked out at Kennedi pitifully, and I couldn't believe it. I wanted to say or do something in my friend's defense, but these girls looked rough and the last thing I wanted to do was to get caught up in some street drama with these hood chicks.

"Kennedi, let's just go," I told her as I took her arm and tried to push her toward the car.

She broke free and stepped back toward the porch. "So, you just gon' stay here?" she yelled at Kendrick.

"You better get her," Kendrick said, backing up against the wall.

It was at that moment that I noticed her torn clothes. I looked at her ripped shirt, then looked at him.

"Did you hit her?" I found myself asking Kendrick.

That suddenly made her want to leave. "Just come on, Maya, let's go," Kennedi said, pulling me toward the car. I debated whether to challenge him some more, but finally I just decided to go ahead and get the heck up out of there. I followed Kennedi back to the car and as soon as we got in and I pulled away I said, "You want to tell me what that was about?"

She was sitting there, sniffling. "He's not answering my

phone calls, but he's sitting up there chillin' with his friend and some girls."

"Was he *with* one of the girls?" I asked.

"He claims they were just sitting there talking."

"Then why wasn't he answering your calls?"

" 'Cause he's a jerk."

We rode in silence for a few minutes, and then I said, "Kennedi, what's the real deal?" I looked over at her in the passenger seat. "I mean, why are you acting like this with him?"

Slow tears trickled down her face again. "I don't know—like, for real I don't know. He just makes me crazy."

"That's not good," I said, looking at my friend sympathetically. "I mean, it's like I don't even know you, the way you're acting."

"Just drop it, okay?" She used the back of her hand to wipe her face.

"I am not going to drop it," I told her. "I refuse to sit around and watch my best friend be abused."

She didn't look at me when she said, "He doesn't abuse me."

I coughed and when she turned to face me, my eyes made my way down to her ripped blouse.

"We had a little tussle, that's all," she said, fixing her shirt as she shifted in the passenger seat.

"You don't rip clothes like that in just a tussle," I told her.

Kennedi rolled her eyes, and the look on her face told me she wished I would just be quiet.

"Did he hit you, Kennedi?" I asked point-blank. I knew he had, but I needed to hear her say it. Better yet, I needed her to hear her say it.

"Maya—"

"Did he hit you?" I repeated. Her silence was my answer, and I had to lean back in my seat in shock. Mynique Foxx was one thing, but watching my BFF in an abusive relationship—that was another thing entirely.

"You know that's completely unacceptable," I finally said.

"Just stay out of it, okay, Maya? I got this," she huffed.

"Obviously, you don't."

"Maya, I'm for real. Mind your business and leave me and my boyfriend alone. This is between me and him." The tone of her voice was firm. And she sounded like she had an attitude. How she was gonna be mad at me was beyond me. She needed to be mad at the lying, cheating, woman beater.

I dropped it for the moment because I could tell Kennedi was upset, but she was crazier than I thought if she even began to *think* I was just going to leave this issue alone. No, she might be temporarily insane, but it was my duty to bring her back to her senses.

Chapter 18

I guess Sheridan couldn't stay mad at me long either because she was standing in front of me, like she hadn't been ignoring me for the past few days.

"So you talking to me now?" I asked.

She hunched her shoulders. "Look, Maya, I don't want to fight with you. I just want you to respect my relationship."

"Fine. Whatever," I told her.

She studied me for a minute, then said, "What is wrong with you?"

I jumped. I hadn't even realized that Sheridan was still standing next to my locker.

"Nothing," I said, as I closed my locker and slung my messenger bag over my shoulder.

"Doesn't look like nothing," she said. "Not with the way you're slamming that locker."

"It's just Kennedi." *And you*, I wanted to add. But I wasn't in the mood to fight with her anymore. I'd dropped Kennedi off last night, and when I'd called to check on her later, she wouldn't answer. The whole situation with both of them was absolutely exhausting.

"What's going on with Kennedi?" Sheridan asked.

I debated telling her, but I knew Kennedi would have a stroke, so I just said, "The usual."

Sheridan shrugged like she couldn't be bothered. "Hey, did you see the new girl, Nelly Fulton?"

"Why would I care about some new chick?"

"Because it's Nelly Fulton, the winner from *The X Factor* last season."

I turned to Sheridan. "Really? That girl can blow? Why is she here?"

"Apparently, her parents insisted that she finish high school, and since her manager is here, they moved here."

I shook my head. "Parents mooching off their kid. Whatever," I replied.

"Well, they're not the only one. Karrington White has attached herself at the hip to Nelly."

I spun around to face Sheridan. "And I care about this, because?"

Sheridan looked taken aback. "I'm sorry. Did someone not have her latte this morning?"

I inhaled. She was trying to make up with me. I just needed to drop it. "Nah, I'm sorry. I didn't mean to snap. It's just that . . ." I didn't get to finish my sentence because Javier came stomping toward us.

Sheridan grinned like a stupid lovesick girl, but quickly lost her smile when she saw the look on his face.

"Hey, babe, what's up?" he asked.

"Did you turn in my paper?" he snapped.

Sheridan dug in her bag. "You said it wasn't due till seventh period." She fished a paper out and handed it to him.

Javier snatched the paper. "You stupid broad! I said second period. I said get it to my teacher by second period."

My mouth fell open in shock. Sheridan wasn't a fighter, but she wasn't a punk either, so I knew she was about to tell him about himself.

"Second? I'm so sorry. I . . . I thought you said seventh," she stammered.

"Ugh!" He scanned the paper. "Maybe if you wasn't always running your mouth." He waved the paper at her. "You lucky, Mr. Warren likes me and gave me thirty minutes to turn this in. I'd better get an A on this paper."

"Javier, I'm so sorry," Sheridan said. But if he heard her, he didn't act like it. He looked at her in disgust, then turned and stomped off.

Sheridan actually stood in the middle of the hallway and began to cry.

I finally snapped myself out of my daze. "Are you freakin' kidding me?" I said. "Are you seriously going to let him talk to you like that?"

"He's just upset. This was an important paper." She dabbed her eyes. "I can't believe I got that wrong."

"If it's so important, why are you doing it?" I asked.

"Maya, don't start."

I shook my head, still in shock. "Wow. Just wow. Are you the same girl that broke up with Lincoln in the tenth grade because he called you a nerd? And you let this dude call you a stupid broad and it's okay?"

"You just don't like Javier," she protested.

"You doggone right, I don't," I replied. "And I don't understand how you can either."

She wiped her tears some more. "You don't need to understand. Maybe if you found a guy you really loved, you'd understand that couples argue."

I didn't miss her low blow and I was definitely going to call her on that—at another time. Right now, I needed to convince her to go get her head examined.

"That wasn't an argument, Sheridan. An argument is when two people go back and forth. He went off. You just stood there. You have let him slob all over you like you're some kind of thirsty, dirty chick. You let him talk to you like you're gutter trash. Don't you have more respect for yourself?"

"Don't you dare judge me," she snapped, suddenly getting angry. "Like you haven't done anything stupid for love. I know what I'm doing and you need to get your own love life and stay out of mine."

The bell rang, giving her a reason to bounce. "Bye," she said, stomping off before I could say another word.

Chapter 19

I was stretched out across my bed, trying my best to concentrate on these figures in front of me. But I noticed that on question number six, Use the limit definition to compute the derivative $f'(x)$. I'd written in the blank, *Who gives a crap?*

Yep, that meant it was time to shut it down. I would have to beg for an extension tomorrow or find someone's paper to copy off of. I hated doing that because then people felt like you owed them something, but I didn't have any other choice because my mind wasn't processing any of this gibberish.

"Knock, knock." My mother stuck her head in the door as she lightly tapped on the door. I wanted to ask her what was the purpose of her knocking if she was just going to come in before I gave her permission. But since my mother wasn't always bougie (every now and then, she could let a little crazy slip out), I didn't say anything.

"Hey," I said, closing my calculus book.

"I was just letting you know that your dad is with your aunt Beverly now."

"How's Travis?" I said, sitting up on the side of my bed.

"He's not doing too well," my mom said as she sat down

next to me. "They're not thinking Beverly will make it through the week."

"Wow," I said. I didn't spend a lot of time around my aunt, but she was super sweet to me. So, this news made me really sad.

My mom shook her head. "That trifling boyfriend of hers, though."

"What about him?" I asked. I didn't know much about the guy my aunt was dating. I just knew my dad despised him as much as Travis did.

"He's at the hospital trying to get her to sign a will," my mom said. "One I'm sure he threw together. Can you believe that?"

"Who is this guy?" I was surprised that Travis hadn't told me much about him. He'd mentioned him a time or two. I knew he didn't like the guy, but he never went into details.

"Some trifling guy she started dating before she got sick," my mom replied.

"You don't think he beat Aunt Beverly up, do you? I mean, could that be why she got sick?"

My mother squinted in my direction. "What? Where'd you get that from?"

I sighed and fell back against my headboard. I couldn't believe that crazy thought had just popped in my head. "I don't know. But are you sure?"

"Yeah, sweetie. Your aunt has cancer. Nobody beat her up." My mother eyed me suspiciously. "Um, this wouldn't have anything to do with your show the other day, would it?" she asked.

"No. I mean, maybe." I shrugged. "It's still on my mind. After the show, this girl called me and said seeing it gave her the strength to leave."

"Wow," my mom said. She patted my thigh as she smiled.

"I love hearing stuff like that. It makes the whole gossip show worthwhile."

"Yeah, I never thought I'd get to someone like that, but it hammered home the fact that there are a lot of people in abusive relationships. I can't believe . . ." I bit my tongue because I didn't want to put Sheridan and Kennedi's business out there like that, but I really did want to get her take on what I should do. I'd debated telling their parents, but I knew snitching to parents was an unforgiveable act. "I just can't believe people, especially teens, would let themselves be caught up in an abusive relationship," I finally said.

"Yeah," my mom said, "I think it's something like one in three teens will be in an abusive relationship before the age of eighteen. It's a real epidemic."

I had to stop and take a second look at my mom. I hadn't thought she knew anything other than the latest fashion trend. She must've read my mind because she laughed. "Sweetie, I know you think your mother is shallow, but I do have a good head on my shoulders. I didn't get my degree in business administration for nothing."

"Wow . . ."

"And, besides, one of the charities I work with deals with domestic abuse."

"Really?" I said. "I didn't know that."

"Because you have no interest in anything that I do," she said, playfully wagging her manicured finger at me.

I smiled. "That's because I thought you didn't do anything but shop."

She stood up. "No, darling. In fact, I'm being honored on Friday for my work with the Riverbend House's Dress for Success program for homeless women."

Dang, I was seeing my mom in a whole new light.

"You can be fabulous and still fight for a cause," she told me.

I thought about what she was telling me. Finally, I said, "My producer, Dexter, said unless I can find some more celebrities getting beat up, he doesn't want to explore the issue of domestic abuse anymore."

"Well, I think this just might be one of those things you have to fight for," my mom replied. "You have a voice, Maya. You should use it."

I knew she was right. Or, on second thought, maybe she wasn't. I did have a voice and I had a lot of followers, and a lot of people who listened to me. But apparently, the two people who mattered most to me weren't trying to hear anything that I said.

"You keep doing what you're doing," my mother said, heading toward my bedroom door. "I'm proud of you."

"Thanks, Mom," I said as she walked out the door.

I fell back on the bed as her words swirled in my head. *One in three teens will be in an abusive relationship.* Me, Sheridan, and Kennedi. The odds already weren't in our favor.

My mother was right. I'd used my voice for a lot of things—to tell a lot of folks' business. I needed to use it now, because it might be the only thing that could save my BFFs from becoming a statistic.

Chapter 20

Google was a beautiful thing. I clicked PRINT on my computer screen and waited for the pages to print out. I plucked the sheets from the printer and stared at the mug shot some more. Apparently, Kendrick Simmons had been arrested last year on domestic abuse charges just days after his eighteenth birthday so his records weren't sealed. He'd gotten off on probation, but the proof that he was abusive was right here in black and white. I don't know why I hadn't thought to Google him back when I was looking up all that stuff on Demond.

I stuffed the papers in my Birkin bag, slipped on my shoes, and headed to Kennedi's to break the news. I'd triple-checked to make sure there were no more cases of mistaken identity. There was no doubt about it; this was Kennedi's man. If this wasn't enough to get my friend to leave Kendrick alone, I didn't know what was.

Twenty minutes later, I was standing in front of Kennedi's mom, who seemed grateful to see me.

"Maya," she said, hugging me. She had on her signature Michael Kors velour sweat suit (I swear, that woman has one of those things in every color).

"Come in," she said, stepping aside and motioning for me to come in. "I have no idea what's going on with my daughter, but maybe you can cheer her up."

"Hi, Mrs. Laura. I'll try." I headed down the hallway to Kennedi's room. Even though they had just moved in, her mom had already had the entire house fixed up. Photos of Kennedi from birth on lined the hallway. The smell of lavender—her mother's favorite fragrance—drifted through the air. I stopped just outside of Kennedi's door, which was tightly closed, and knocked.

"Come in," Kennedi called out.

I gently eased the door open. The room was pitch black. Kennedi was sitting on the bed, like she'd just been sitting there staring out into space. "Hey, K. You up?"

"Yeah," she said, pulling her legs up underneath her and tossing her phone on the bed.

"Your mom let me in." I flipped on the light. "What are you doing sitting up in here in the dark?"

She stared at her phone. "Just trying to text Kendrick. He's not responding."

I took a deep breath. I was starting to think maybe my friend was mentally ill. I'd heard of being lovesick, but I didn't know it was real.

"Well, that's actually what I wanted to talk to you about," I said, sitting on the edge of the bed.

"Maya, please don't start," Kennedi said, getting up and walking away from me.

"I'm not trying to start anything. You're my girl and I care about you and I don't want to see you hurt."

"I'm not hurt," she finally said.

"Obviously, you're sitting here in the dark, going crazy." I sighed, then lowered my voice. "Did sleeping with him make you like this?"

Slow tears trickled down her cheeks. I swear, I'd seen my

friend cry more in this past month than I had since I'd known her.

"You know I was saving myself," she said.

I walked up behind her and rubbed her back. "Okay, I get that. But it's no need to lose your mind over him."

"I love him," she said, not looking at me.

"Love doesn't hurt," I told her. "And if you're dating an abuser . . ."

She moved away from me. "He's not an abuser."

"Kennedi, you forget—I saw. Your clothes were ripped. He was struggling to contain his anger. I see how violent this relationship is." I took a deep breath, then reached in my purse, pulled out the piece of paper, and handed it to her. "And then, there's this."

"What is that?" she said, reaching out to take the paper. She studied the paper for a minute. "Are you investigating my boyfriend?" she screamed.

I held up my hand to stop her. "Before you flip out, let me explain. I only did it because I'm worried about you."

She stomped away from me, furious.

"Really, Maya? How 'bout you mind your own freakin' business?" She tore the paper in half, balled it up, and tossed it at me as she said, "Oh, I forgot, you don't know how!"

I stared at her as the paper fluttered to the floor.

"Really, K?"

"I can't believe you!"

I couldn't believe how upset she was getting. I pointed to the paper on the floor. "And you think that's going to make it better?" I asked. "You think tearing up his mug shot is going to make the fact that he likes to hit girls go away?"

"You think you know everything!" she spat at me. "I knew about the arrest! It wasn't even like that."

Now, I really was speechless. Kennedi knew? She actually knew that her boyfriend had been arrested for domestic assault and she didn't see anything wrong with it?

"Are you serious?" I finally asked. "So, you're okay with dating an abusive guy?"

"Leave it alone!" She walked over and grabbed my purse and thrust it at me. "I'm tired. I'll talk to you later."

"Seriously, K? You're kicking me out?"

"Bye, Maya. I just want to be left alone."

I just stood, staring at her. "We were supposed to be going to the movies." Even when Kennedi had agreed earlier to go to the movies, I'd known she was going to find a way to bail on me.

"I don't feel like it." She held my purse out again until I took it.

"Fine, whatever," I said, stomping toward the door. I didn't get it. Kendrick was the one laying hands on her. Kendrick was the one not answering her calls. Kendrick was the one giving her major grief. So, why in the world was Kennedi mad at me?

Chapter 21

I was so glad to have today off. I'd had to put on a smile and fake the funk at a movie premiere last night. The movie sucked, but it was starring one of my friends, model Savannah Vanderpool, in her acting debut. She'd come a long way in a fight against drugs, so I didn't know how I was going to rip her movie to shreds.

Then, I had to go to a party after the premiere, so I didn't get home until two in the morning. Then, I had to get to school on time because I had a test first period, so I'd been dragging all day. I was ready to get home, but I needed to get to the gym and turn in my health report. I didn't do gyms because the last thing I was going to do was run up and down a court, sweating out my Brazilian blowout, so I'd been excused. But part of being excused included doing these stupid research papers, which to me were just a frivolous waste of time. They weren't that hard, just an inconvenience.

I had just taken a short cut through the girls' locker room when I saw something that made me stop in my tracks. Javier was going through one of the lockers. He was the only person in there, but I could hear the girls' basketball team practicing in the gym.

I stood back and watched him as he picked the lock, then casually opened the locker and started going through the stuff like it was his. I saw him pick up what looked like an iPhone and drop it in his pocket. He closed that locker and moved to the one right next to it. I started scrambling for my phone. Okay, maybe he wasn't a cheater, but he was definitely a thief. And there was no twin mess this go-round. Javier still had on that lame plaid shirt I'd seen him in earlier.

As soon as I got the phone out of my pocket, though, it fell to the floor. I scrambled to try and catch it, but couldn't. Luckily, it was in an OtterBox case, so the phone wasn't damaged, but my cover was definitely blown.

I looked up to see Javier staring at me. "Is there something I can help you with?" he asked.

I clutched my phone. "You find what you were looking for in that locker?" I asked.

He glared at me, and if looks could kill, I had no doubt I'd be straight-up dead right about now.

"You're such a pain," he said, stepping closer to me, "always scrambling around, spying on people."

"Boy, no one was spying on you. I just so happened to be coming through when I saw you breaking into these lockers."

He actually leaned back and smiled. "I wasn't breaking into nothing. My friend forgot her code and asked me to come in here and get something for her."

"What friend?"

"Not that it's any of your business, but Gina."

"Who is that?" I asked. "I've never even heard of someone named Gina?"

"You don't know everyone that goes here," he protested.

"Whatever." I pushed him aside. "Let's see what Coach Wilson thinks about you breaking into girls' lockers."

He grabbed my arm as I tried to pass him and slammed me up against the door.

"Have you lost your mind?" I said, jerking my hand away.

I don't know why Javier didn't scare me, but he didn't. I felt like he was all talk. I took a step toward him. "I'm not your little girlfriend. If you ever put your hands on me again, I promise you will regret it."

"You rich chicks think you're all that," he sneered.

"Yeah, you sure are slobbin' after one of those rich chicks."

He grinned. "Correction, that rich chick is slobbin' after me. And I have her right where I want her."

"Ugh, you're so disgusting. I can't wait to tell Sheridan what you said."

"Go ahead and snitch. It's your word against mine about everything. And trust, I can get someone to vouch for me. Shoot, I can get your BFF to vouch for me."

I glared at him but didn't reply because the sad part was, he probably could. Sheridan's nose was so wide open that she would probably lie for this jerk.

"Oh, *you* trust, I'll make sure that Sheridan knows that she's dating a thief."

That made him lose his smile. "I don't need to steal anything." He grinned again. "I have a rich girlfriend that will buy me whatever my heart desires."

"Good, maybe she can put some money on your books when you're in jail."

"I can't stand you," he said.

"The feeling is mutual," I replied, turning to head to the coach's office.

"Oh, and just so you know, my girl has told me some things you might not want getting out," he called out after me.

I don't know why, but I stopped in my tracks as I wracked my brain for anything that I'd done that could get me in any major trouble. Yeah, Sheridan and I had done a lot of things over the years, but nothing that could get us in any major trouble. Except . . . Naw, I shook that thought away. No way would Sheridan have ever shared that.

Or would she?

"I know how you guys set up Kary White. I know about those dresses you took on a dare." He flashed a wicked smile. "I know a whole lot."

I didn't know if he was bluffing or what, but I turned and kept walking.

"Open your big mouth and I promise you'll be sorry," he called out after me.

I turned back to face him. "I don't do threats."

"But I do," he replied matter-of-factly. "I'm a scholarship kid from the other side of the tracks, remember? It would be a shame for something to happen to that fine mama of yours."

The look in his eyes actually sent a flutter of fear through me. But I managed not to let it show.

"Whatever, Javier. I'm out, so you can keep breaking in lockers."

I left the gym, but Javier's threat had sent a chill up my spine. Instead of heading left to go to Coach Wilson's office, I turned right to go home.

Chapter 22

I knew that I should've gone to Coach Wilson and reported Javier, but I didn't need any extra drama. I already had it where my bodyguard, Mann, didn't come with me to school. I wanted to keep it that way. I didn't want to be in fear even when I was going to class. Besides, I needed to talk to Sheridan first and find out exactly what she'd told that fool.

I kept one hand on the steering wheel as I dialed her number for the fifth time. And for the fifth time, it went straight to voice mail.

Finally, I gave up. I scrolled through my phone until I found the phone number for Sheridan's aunt, Cora. Cora lived in the house with Sheridan and was supposed to be watching her while her mother worked. Ms. Matthews was in France now on a six-week movie shoot.

"Hi, Ms. Cora, it's Maya," I said when she answered.

"Hey, sweetie," she sang. I actually liked Ms. Cora. She loved having fun and was always in a good mood. But I guess you could be when you didn't have to work, didn't have any kids of your own, and got to live the high life off of your sister's money.

"Are you in town?" I asked.

"Yeah, baby. But not for long. Heading to Vegas for a girls' weekend." She sounded like she was in her convertible—a top-of-the-line Jag—because it was hard to hear her.

"Well, I was trying to see if you're at home. I'm really trying to catch up with Sheridan."

"I'm not at home, but I just left about five minutes ago."

"Was she there?"

"Speak up, baby. I can't hear you. No, you know what? Hold on. Let me put the top up."

I waited a few minutes, and then she came back on the line. "Now, what were you saying?"

"I said, I'm trying to find Sheridan. Was she at home when you left?"

"Yeah. She was there. In there on the phone with that boy. Shoot, she stays on the phone with that boy. I tried to tell her, no beautiful young woman like her needs to be tied up with a boy like that. She needs to be footloose and fancy-free. Plus, when she does date, she needs to date someone on her own level. She keeps dating this gutter trash. Most of these guys are just after her money. I don't know why that girl is so gung ho on having a boyfriend. She acts like something is wrong if she doesn't have some boy sniffing behind her. Probably because of her daddy issues." She tsked. "If she knows like I know, she'll enjoy the single life for the rest of her life."

I knew Ms. Cora would ramble on and on if I didn't stop her.

"Okay, Ms. Cora. I was just asking because I was trying to get in touch with her. It's kinda important."

"You called her?"

"Yes, but she's not answering."

"Hmph, probably because she won't click over when he's on the phone, talking about he doesn't like to be put on hold. What kind of mess is that? I tried to tell her, but of course, she won't listen to me."

If Sheridan was at home and not answering, then that meant that she was probably talking to Javier. That meant that he was trying to come up with some story to cover his tracks.

"All right, Ms. Cora. I'll keep trying her."

"Okay, baby. Why don't you come and stay with Sheridan this weekend? I hate her being in that big ol' house by herself."

I wanted to tell Ms. Cora that was what Ms. Matthews paid her for, but I didn't feel like getting cussed out, so I just said, "I just may do that."

"Great. Okay, sweetie, I'll talk to you later. I'm at the spa and they will try to give my spot away if I'm late."

I said good-bye, then hung up the phone. I immediately sent Sheridan a text.

Call me!!!

Five minutes later, when she still hadn't answered, I texted her again.

Don't believe his lies!!!

Three minutes later, I was about to send another text when my phone rang and Sheridan's picture popped up on the screen.

"Hello," I said.

"Maya, what is your problem?"

I could hear the attitude in Sheridan's voice, and I could tell that this conversation was not going to go well.

I pulled over into a Starbucks parking lot. "So, let me guess. Your boyfriend had a perfectly good explanation as to why he was breaking into girls' lockers?"

"Really, Maya? Breaking into lockers? He didn't break into anything."

"How do you know, Sheridan? Were you there? No, you weren't. But I was. And yes, he was breaking into lockers."

I could just see her rolling her eyes. "Yeah, just like he was at Sullivan's Steakhouse with some chick."

"Okay, so I was wrong about that, but I'm not wrong about this. He's such a prick. And what did you tell him about us?"

"What do you mean?" she replied.

"Javier said that you told him all the stuff we did together, like when we made Kary White think Jock wanted to go out with her."

"I told him some stuff. Just silly stuff we did back in the day. What's the big deal?" She actually sounded agitated.

I wanted to ask her why she was even discussing me with him, since he didn't like me and I didn't like him. "Oh, I know what you're thinking," she finally said. "Don't worry, I didn't tell him *that*. Some of us have respect for our friendship," she sarcastically added.

"And just what is that supposed to mean?"

"Exactly what I said." She huffed. "Maya, the bottom line is, as much as you'd like to make him out to be one, Javier isn't a thief."

"When did you get to be so dumb?" The words were out of my mouth before I even realized it. I'm sure that caught her by surprise because silence filled the phone until I said, "Sheridan, I'm sorry."

"No," she said, angrily. "This dumb chick is done talking to you about her man. Yes, Javier had a perfectly good explanation. But it's none of your business what that was. In fact, nothing of what I do is your business. I don't know what it's going to take to get that through your thick skull. This job got you messed up. You don't know how to stay out of other people's business. But let me make this very clear—I don't want your advice, I don't need your input, and I don't want to hear anything else you have to say about my boyfriend."

The next sound I heard was the phone hanging up in my ear. I just sat in my car staring at my phone, I was so dumb-founded. So, Sheridan could get some spunk and stand up to me, but she couldn't stand up to that loser she was dating. I'll admit, I shouldn't have called her dumb, but that stuff she just said was out of order.

She was lucky, though. Her aunt Cora's words rang in my ears. I was starting to believe there was some truth to what she said. Sheridan's mom stayed gone all the time. There was some big secret as to who her dad was. Ms. Matthews wouldn't admit it, but there was a rumor that he was a big-time married movie producer. So, Sheridan longed to be loved, by any means necessary. That was the only explanation as to why she would be into someone like Javier. And so, for that reason, I was going to let her make it. I was mad, but I'd let her make it.

I had just pulled back on the freeway when my phone rang again. Kennedi's picture popped up. I wondered if Sheridan had called her.

"Hello," I said.

"Hello," she said, sniffing. As soon as I heard her, I knew this call had nothing to do with Sheridan.

"Hey, Kennedi. What's wrong?" I asked, even though I already knew the answer. Only one thing made her cry these days. He was about six feet tall with light gray eyes and liked to beat on girls.

"What's always wrong with me?" Kennedi said.

I took a deep breath. "So, what did he do this time?"

"He broke up with me. I think it's for real this time," she sobbed.

I wanted to say, "Good." I rolled my eyes and tried to think of something more tactful to say. "Well, maybe it's for the best."

"Whatever, Maya."

So much for my old BFF being back. I guessed Kennedi was back to trippin'. I hated the fact that I had no idea what

mood she would be in these days and it was all behind yet another loser.

"Where are you?" she asked.

"Going home." I sighed in frustration. "I just saw Sheridan's
trifling boyfriend breaking into a locker in the girls' gym."

"Really?" she asked, even though it sounded like she
couldn't care less.

"I tried to tell her, but she just got mad and told me that
I needed to mind my own business."

Kennedi didn't reply.

"So, I guess you agree with what she said."

"I don't even know what she said, Maya."

"I told you. She said the show has me thinking that it's
okay to get in people's business."

She blew a frustrated breath. "I've been telling you that.
You and your two cents have really gotten old."

I was sick of being the bad guy, especially when all I was
trying to do was help. "You know what? If you and Sheridan
want to stay in these jacked-up relationships, do you," I
snapped.

"At least we got a relationship," she snapped back.

I wanted to remind her that really, she didn't, but I just
said, "I'm sorry. I'd rather be by myself than be in a relationship where I'm being abused."

"I don't get abused," she protested. "You know what,
Maya? I'm with Sheridan—since you got this little show, you
think you're the queen of everything. And you think you
have a right to be in everybody's business. Well, you don't
have a right to dictate who I see, who Sheridan sees, or anything we do with our lives. Get your own life and stop wor-
rying about ours." And for the second time that day, one of
my best friends hung up on me.

Chapter 23

I was headed to see the one person who hadn't lost their mind—Alvin. As soon as I got off the phone with Kennedi, I called and told him that I was on my way over. He sounded a little distracted, but he was going to have to refocus and help me figure out what to do. I navigated my BMW off the exit ramp that led to Alvin's house. I pulled in to his driveway and made my way up to his sidewalk. Alvin met me at the front door, a look of concern on his face.

"Are you okay?" he asked. "You sound stressed."

"No, I'm not okay," I replied.

He reached out and, without saying a word, pulled me into a tight bear hug. I wish that I liked Alvin like that because he always made me feel so safe, but that wasn't what I was here for.

"I need to vent," I said, pulling away.

"Just call me the ventilator," he said, grinning as he motioned for me to come in.

"You are so corny." I laughed as I walked in, then set my purse on the coffee table and looked around. "Where's your mom?"

"Upstairs in her room. Where she always is."

He was right about that. Since I'd known Alvin, I'd only met his mom three or four times. At first, I'd thought it was crazy that a twenty-one-year-old guy as rich as Alvin lived with his mother, but then I'd found out that she actually lived with him. She'd been sick so Alvin had bought the house outright and moved her in.

"So, what's up?" Alvin asked after we had gotten settled in the living room.

I sighed. "Kennedi and Sheridan have both lost their minds."

"Still boy trouble?" he asked, taking my purse off my shoulder.

I nodded. "And it's like they've been smoking that K2 or something that was going around last month."

He laughed. "I doubt your friends are doing any drugs."

I used to think that, but I didn't know what to think about them anymore. "I don't know what else can explain how they've lost their minds," I said.

"So you said something on the phone about Kendrick being arrested for domestic abuse."

"Yeah," I said. I pulled out another copy of Kendrick's mug shot since Kennedi had torn up the first one. "Look at this. He was arrested less than a year ago for assaulting his girlfriend, and Kennedi doesn't even care about that."

"Wow," Alvin said, studying the piece of paper. "I can't believe she's attracted to a guy like this."

"Yeah, you and me both, especially since Kennedi was always the strong one of the group, the one who didn't take any mess. How she's able to allow herself to be in an abusive relationship is beyond me."

"Do you know for a fact that she's being abused?" he asked, handing the paper back to me.

"Yes." I tucked the paper back into my bag. "I mean maybe he's not beating her up, per se but he's definitely laying his hands on her. The other night she came from the back where they had been fighting and her clothes were ripped. She was crying and he was pissed. And he had his fists balled up like he was ready to punch her."

"Wow," Alvin said.

"And then, there's Sheridan. She's not any better. Javier may not have laid any hands on her, but he's definitely verbally abusing her."

"Well, you know a lot of people don't see words as abuse," Alvin replied. "I had a cousin who talked to his girl so bad, we had to tell him about himself. He looked at us like we were crazy when we told him that was abuse."

"Yeah, that's how Javier is. If he talks to her crazy in front of people, I can only imagine what he does when they're alone." I shook my head. "I just can't believe the way he talks to her and the fact that she allows it."

"I'm shocked," Alvin said. Of course, he'd met both Sheridan and Kennedi, but he really knew them through all the things I shared.

"You're shocked? How do you think *I* feel? But that's not even the worst of it."

I then replayed what I had caught Javier doing in the girls' locker room.

"So, he's a thief, too?" Alvin asked in disbelief.

"Yes, and what's so jacked up is I tried to tell Sheridan, and Javier once again beat me to her, making it out like I was lying. I just can't believe this. We've been friends since like, forever, and she takes his word over mine."

"Dang," Alvin replied. "So, what are you gonna do?"

"I don't know. When I try to talk to the two of them, neither one of them is trying to hear what I'm saying and they're making it out like *I'm* the one who's crazy, and I'm the one who's out of order for 'butting in,' as Sheridan said."

"You know sometimes, you have to let people make their own mistakes," he said.

"Yeah, I get that, but I can't sit back and do nothing," I said.

"So again, then, what are you going to do?"

I shifted on the sofa. I had thought about this all the way over here. "That's what I wanted to talk to you about," I told him. "I need to do something. I tried talking and it's not helping. But I can't just sit back and watch my best friends be in abusive relationships."

"Do you think you should tell their parents?" he asked.

I stood and started pacing. "I don't know. Neither one of them would forgive me for that, plus Kennedi's parents are already trippin' because they're worried about her. They'd probably ground her until she was twenty-five."

"That's a tough one."

"Yeah, tell me about it." Before I could say anything else, Alvin's doorbell rang. He looked at me uneasily, but didn't move. The bell rang again.

"Aren't you going to get that?"

He just stared at me.

"Who is it?" I asked.

"I, um . . . I was kind of um . . ."

I looked at him and raised an eyebrow. "Why don't you want to answer your door?"

"That's, um . . . that's Marisol. She was . . ."

I didn't give him time to finish. I stomped over to the door. I couldn't even get time with him without Marisol popping up.

I swung the door open and the big, cheesy grin quickly evaporated from her face.

"So, that's your car?" she said, attitude all over her face.

I'd met Marisol many times, and although she tried to act nice to me, it was so fake it was ridiculous. I could tell that she didn't like me. But it's not like I cared. I didn't like her either. Alvin was a nice guy, and Marisol looked like she'd been around the block a few times. She was so thirsty, and I couldn't believe Alvin was attracted to her.

Alvin moved to the door before either of us could say a word.

"Hey, Marisol," he said, motioning for her to come in.

She immediately plastered a smile back on. "Hey, baby," she said, leaning in to kiss him on the lips. I could tell it caught him by surprise. Marisol walked in, then turned to face me. "Hey, Maya. What are you doing here?"

I was about to tell her none of her business, but Alvin jumped in.

"Maya just stopped by for a minute."

I cut my eyes at Alvin. Why in the heck was he acting so nervous?

"Oh, that's sweet." She turned to Alvin. "But we're going to be late for the game."

I looked at Alvin. "What game? You didn't say you were about to leave."

"Oh, my boo got us floor seats for the Heat–Lakers game," Marisol answered for him. She draped her arm through his. "He is always spoiling me." She held out her arm in my direction. "Like this diamond tennis bracelet he got me for my birthday last week. Isn't it gorgeous?"

I swear, I felt sick to my stomach. If Alvin was buying her diamonds and getting her floor seats to NBA games, this relationship was more serious than he was letting on.

"Wow" was all I could say.

"Well, I guess you should be running along," Marisol told me. "Alvin, tell your little friend bye."

Marisol stood there grinning like she'd really put me in my place.

"Little?" I said, folding my arms.

"Maya, she's right." Alvin once again jumped in between us. "We need to get going. We can catch up later."

My gaze went from Alvin—who was so nervous he was sweating like it was the middle of summer—to Marisol, who still was looking smug.

"Don't bother," I finally said, grabbing my purse. "You go do you, Alvin and I'll keep doing me."

I turned and hightailed it out of there before I found myself in the middle of any more trouble.

Chapter 24

Okay, so I might have been wrong about Javier breaking into a locker. As it turns out, Kayla, a freshman who lived in his apartment complex, really did call and ask him to get her phone out of the locker. She'd come up to me at school yesterday to let me know since Javier must've told her what I'd accused him of.

Truthfully, ol' girl might've even been lying, but it still made me look bad. Though I dang sure didn't *feel* bad. Javier might have had permission to go in that one locker, but I'd seen him go in more than one. So, I have no doubt that if I hadn't gone in there, Javier would've cleaned out the rest of those lockers and robbed the girls' basketball team blind.

Even still, I hated that he now had some ammunition to convince Sheridan that I just wanted to break them up. Of course, nothing could be further from the truth. I wanted my girl to be happy. Just with someone that deserved her.

I pushed aside thoughts of that jerk and returned to my work. Digging up dirt and gossip was hard. I'd just finished checking all the blogs, looking through the latest tabloids, and following up with my sources, trying to find the next major story. Because I'd done everything from exposing the infamous K2 drug ring to tracking down an Internet imposter, I felt like every show had to top the next, and right about now it seemed like my well was running dry. I leaned back in my chair and stretched, and just as I did Yolanda, my assistant, walked in.

"Hey, are you watching TV?" She had a panicked expression on her face.

"No, why? What's going on?" I leaned up and flipped on the television at the end of my dressing table.

"Turn to CNN."

I flipped over as the anchor was talking. *"Again, if you're just tuning in, CNN has learned that actress Mynique Foxx has died."*

"What?" I said, my mouth falling open. "What happened?"

"Listen," Yolanda said, pointing at the TV.

"The search continues for the man police believe is responsible for her murder."

Demond Cash's picture flashed on the screen and I thought I was going to pass out.

"CNN has learned," the anchor continued, *"that Cash is expected to turn himself in to authorities later today. We'll stay on top of this story and keep you updated."*

"Wow," I said, pushing the mute button as they went to commercial. "What happened?"

Yolanda shrugged. "I don't know. They said there was a fight outside of a club last night, and then police found her body this morning. Apparently the housekeeper found her or something and called police."

"Wow," I repeated. "How do they know Demond did it?"

"Because the housekeeper said he had blood on his shirt and he fled as soon as she walked in. They said she had been shot."

"Shot?" I exclaimed.

"Yeah. In the stomach."

I couldn't do anything but shake my head. I'd tried to help the girl and she'd turned on me. Now look at where she was. "So, what happened?" I asked.

"I don't know," Yolanda shrugged. "I was just watching it in the break room. It sounds like their fight at the club moved home."

Just then, Tamara stuck her head into my office. "Maya, did you see the Mynique Foxx story?"

"Yeah," I told her.

"How did *we* not break that?"

I raised an eyebrow at Tamara. Like I was supposed to know when somebody got killed. "Um, I don't work the police beat. You should be talking to your news department."

Tamara let out a frustrated sigh. "Fine, but I need you to get right on this. See what you can find out about Demond."

I wanted to ask her what did she expect me to get. Demond hated me so there was no way he was going to talk to me. She must've read the look on my face because she said, "Look, just do what you can. I'd like for us to have something fresh when we tape tomorrow."

I sighed. "Okay, I'll get on it." She didn't say anything else as she turned and left my office, no doubt to see what dirt she could dig up herself.

"Anything you need me to do?" Yolanda asked.

"Yeah, can you go in the system and pull up Demond's record, and see if he has any other arrests? Maybe I missed something earlier. If he would get angry enough to shoot someone, this can't be the first time he got into trouble. You might need to go to the news department to see if they can get into the database to find out if there's anything that's been sealed."

"Okay, I'm on it."

My eyes went back to the TV after she left. CNN had moved on to another story.

Mynique Foxx's life had been reduced to sixty seconds on the evening news. If only she had listened.

I turned back to my computer to see if I could find out anything, and my screen saver scrolled across the computer. It was me, Sheridan, and Kennedi. I think that picture was taken at the Miami-Dade County Fair. We didn't do fairs but had decided to crash the event because we hadn't had anything else to do, and it had turned out to be so much fun. Looking at both of my friends and thinking about Mynique Foxx, I knew I had to do something. Mynique hadn't listened. She hadn't wanted my help, and now look where it had gotten her.

No, my BFFs wouldn't end up like Mynique Foxx. Not if I had anything to do about it. And there *was* something I could do. It would give Tamara the ratings she wanted and hopefully serve as a wake-up call to my friends. I just hoped they'd forgive me for doing it.

Chapter 25

News of Mynique Foxx's death was spreading like crazy. She may not have been that popular of an actress, but everybody was talking about her now.

I was sitting in my seventh-period class and Ms. Williams had already had to tell the class twice to stop talking.

I think on any given day Mynique's story might not have been such a big deal to these people, but the fact that Demond Cash was apparently the one who had done it had tongues wagging left and right.

"So, Maya, what's the real scoop?" this girl named Kimmie said, leaning in and whispering behind me.

"How about you tune into my show because right now I'm off duty and trying to get an education?" I said, turning to the front. I really wasn't listening to Ms. Williams and was counting down till the clock struck 3 PM.

"You don't have to be funky," she said, rolling her eyes and leaning back in her seat.

It's crazy. I know that I reported a lot of drama from other people, but I didn't get off by hearing dirt and gossip. I was just doing my job. But it's like these people were just taking some kind of sick pleasure in Mynique's tragedy.

"So, have they arrested him yet?" I heard the girl next to me ask.

"No, he was supposed to turn himself in, but I hear he's on the run," Kimmie replied. "I mean, he is Demond Cash. I don't know how he thinks he's going to run far."

"Wow, that's jacked up," the girl said.

I wanted them both to just be quiet. All I could think was just maybe had I done something differently, maybe if I had followed up on their story, maybe if I'd stopped them that night in the parking lot, maybe Mynique would still be alive.

I shook the thought off. I wasn't to blame. Mynique had put herself in that situation and stayed in that situation.

The bell finally rang and I made my way to my locker. I had to get to the station to see what our researchers had been able to dig up on the Mynique and Demond story. Honestly, though, my heart wasn't in it. But I knew there was no way around it—this would be our top story today.

As soon as I rounded the corner outside my class, I saw Javier and Sheridan once again in what looked like a heated debate. I couldn't make out what they were saying, but as I got closer, he got louder. It was like they were in their own world, oblivious to anyone around them.

"To be so smart, you're one of the dumbest chicks I know," I heard him saying.

"Javier," Sheridan said, her eyes getting watery.

I couldn't do anything but stare at them. I really and truly didn't know what had happened to my girlfriend. Granted, she'd never been the feisty type, but she dang sure wasn't the type to stand around and take this. I pulled out my phone so I could discreetly start recording. If Sheridan wouldn't hear me when I told her how crazy she looked, maybe seeing herself would open her eyes. I took a deep breath, then wondered if I should leave it alone. But before I knew it, I was heading in their direction, my camera clutched upright in my hand so I could record them.

"So, this doesn't ever get old, huh?" I said, approaching them.

"Oh, here *you* come," he said, rolling his eyes. "How about you stay out of our business?"

"Maya, I've got this. Don't worry about it," Sheridan said.

I ignored her. "My best friend *is* my business." I turned to face Sheridan. "What is wrong with you, Sheridan? Why are you taking this from this nobody? He's rude, disrespectful, and a lying thug. He doesn't even have a car!"

"My ride is in the shop," he yelled, "but you don't need to worry about what I got and what I don't got."

"You *don't got* any English skills," I said, rolling my eyes. "Come on, Sheridan."

She pulled away from me. "Maya, chill out. Dang. Mind your own business."

"What is it with this dude?" I said, stunned.

Javier actually had the nerve to pull her in a hug close to him. "This dude loves her and you just hatin' because you don't even know what that is," Javier said.

"Sweetie, if you're any indication of what love is, I'll pass," I said. "I'd rather be single for the rest of my life."

He looked me up and down. "And you probably *will* be! Ol' stuck-up—"

"Javier," Sheridan said, cutting him off.

"Come on, babe. Let's go." He started pulling her away.

"Sheridan." I needed to get through to her. "You deserve better than this. Why are you putting up with this? You can have any guy you want. You don't need this from this clown."

"It's not even like that," she said.

"Yeah, Maya, it's not even like that," Javier added. "Me and my baby had a little spat, but it ain't nothing you need to worry about. You need to worry about getting your own self in order."

I threw my hands up in frustration. I was about to give up. I don't know what was wrong with Sheridan. She'd dated sons of celebrities and dignitaries and all kinds of top-of-the-line dudes wanted her, yet she was settling for this fool!

I didn't know how I could get through to my friends. But I was determined to find out what Javier was holding over my girl because obviously he'd slipped her some kind of drug or something. I was going to do whatever it took to give her a wake-up call.

I'd been going back and forth over whether I really should carry out my plan, but this situation just confirmed it. I was moving full speed ahead, and whatever happened as a result of that would just happen.

Chapter 26

I could tell by the look on Alvin's face he wasn't feeling my idea. After that whole situation with Marisol, I almost hadn't called Alvin. Of course, he'd downplayed their relationship again. But it still made me mad. I had to get over it, though, because I needed someone to talk to. J. Love was on tour and if the conversation didn't involve me or him, he really wasn't trying to hear it. Alvin was the only one I could talk to.

Right about now, I was wishing that I hadn't said anything, but I'd needed to run this idea by someone. This was gonna be major, so I needed someone to tell me I was doing the right thing. I knew that I needed to do whatever I could to save my girls and they might not like it now, but they would thank me later.

"I can't believe you're going to put your girls on blast like that," Alvin said.

"I don't know what else to do," I replied. "I've tried talking to them. I've tried reasoning, but neither one of them thinks they're in a bad situation."

He seemed like he was weighing his words. "Do you

think you should do like they both said and let them make their own mistakes?"

"Yeah, like I did with Mynique," I said matter-of-factly.

He was quiet at that. No, I couldn't stand Mynique Foxx, but I didn't want her dead. And maybe if I hadn't minded my business, she wouldn't be.

"I don't know, Maya, that just seems kind of risky. These are your girls you're talking about."

"What choice do I have?"

A dejected look crossed his face like he knew I was right.

"Okay, I hope it turns out the way that you want."

I could see that if we kept talking about this, he was going to try and change my mind, so I decided to change the subject. Today's show about Mynique—Demond was still on the run—had worn me down. So, I was happy when Alvin asked to take me out to dinner. But, I'd griped and complained about my situation with my girls for the past hour. Now, I just wanted us to laugh and have a good time like we used to.

"So, what's going on with you?" I asked.

"Nothing. Just in talks with Snapchat for this new program I came up with that will make their streamlining a lot easier."

I smiled. He knew I was asking about Marisol, but I didn't press it. Snapchat was the next big thing so I wanted to hear about that. Alvin was a whiz with the computer. He'd dropped out of college. For anyone else, that might have bothered me, but he'd dropped out because he was making so much money doing his computer stuff. He'd never told me how much he'd gotten from his video game patent, but from the way he was rolling in dough, I knew he'd been paid pretty well.

"So, what about you?" he asked. "How's the love life?"

"See, there you go," I laughed. "You want to brush your love life off and ask me about mine."

"Naw, I heard about you and Mr. Superstar at the party."

"What, you spying on me?"

"Girl, please, it was all over the blogs. The Princess and the Prince," he said sarcastically.

"You can't believe everything you read or hear—unless of course, you heard it from *Rumor Central*. You're the one, though. You and your girlfriend," I said, sarcastically. "Big baller."

He shook his head. "It's not even like that. I told you that."

I was just about to say something when Marisol blew into the restaurant like a woman on a mission. She did not look happy.

She stomped over and stopped right in front of our table.

"Marisol," Alvin said, jumping up.

I looked at her, then back at him, then back at her. She was glaring at him like he'd done something wrong.

"This doesn't look like a meeting to me," she snapped.

"Naw, I . . . I was just . . . me and um, Maya, we were just catching up."

I turned up my nose. Why in the world was Alvin acting like he'd done something wrong?

"Umm, hello, Marisol," I said.

She looked over her shoulder at me but didn't speak. *Seriously?*

"Catching up? You just saw her the other day. What do you need to catch up about?" she asked.

"Marisol, now's not the time," Alvin said, looking nervously around.

She ignored him as she continued. "I thought we were going to be open and honest," she said.

I raised a perfectly arched eyebrow in Alvin's direction as I waited on an explanation.

"I, ah . . ."

"Okay, does someone want to explain to me what's going on?" I finally said as the two of them just stood there glaring at each other.

"Well, ah . . ." Alvin began.

Marisol finally turned to me and said, "Well, ah, Alvin and I are together now. Officially and exclusively together."

I was speechless. This was information Alvin didn't feel like I needed to know? They were a couple?

It was my turn to glare at him. "Wow. Well, no. Alvin didn't mention that," I said.

Now we both were glaring at him.

"And why didn't you mention it, Alvin?" Marisol asked. "Especially since you told me that you'd already told her."

I couldn't take anymore. I finally stood up. "You know what, Marisol? Alvin and I are just really good friends. There is no need to feel threatened by me."

She turned her nose up at me. "Oh, trust me, I don't feel threatened by you."

Oh, this chick was for real trippin'. But since I could see she was a little upset, I was going to let her make it. Besides, I was so done with Alvin over this. He'd just sat here and lied to my face.

"Whatever," I said, slinging my hobo bag over my shoulder. "I'm going to let you lovebirds finish this dinner."

Alvin reached out and grabbed my arm. "Maya, let me explain."

I instinctively snatched my arm away. I couldn't believe Alvin had done this. He had no reason to lie to me, yet he did. "Don't."

"No, I just . . ."

I stared at him. "I just thought we were better than that." I turned to Marisol. "He's all yours, boo-boo. Trust and believe, you won't have to worry about me again."

I walked out the restaurant to the sound of Alvin pleading for me to hear him out. Yes, I was angry. But more than anything, I think I was hurt. And if I was hurt, that meant my feelings for Alvin ran much deeper than I ever wanted to admit. I shook away that thought. It didn't matter now. I'd slept on Alvin and it looked like he had moved on.

Chapter 27

I took a deep breath. In. Out. In. Out. We were fifteen seconds away from show time and the point of no return. I had thought about what Alvin said—before Marisol had blown in. I'd thought about all the damage I'd done in the past, and I'd almost changed my mind, but then, I'd thought about Mynique Foxx and how her life had been cut short because I'd left it alone. Yes, I'd aired her story once. I should've followed up and stayed on it. I had been worried about embarrassing her when I should have done whatever it took to get her to see the danger that she was placing herself in. No. I didn't know if I could've saved Mynique Foxx, but if I had done something maybe she'd be alive today. I refused to see my girls go out like that, and if that meant they didn't speak to me for a little while, then that was just a chance I would have to take.

"Stand by, Maya," my director, Manny, said, giving me the cue as the music came up.

I took one last deep breath and then plastered on my smile as the theme music faded out and the red light came on, signaling for me to go.

"What's up, everybody? It's your girl Maya Morgan and

you're tuned into *Rumor Central*, where we dish the dirt on the celebrities you love. And boy, am I dishing it today." I took a deep breath, then continued, "But I'm going to be honest, this isn't an easy story for me to do. You guys know I get down and dirty on this show because somebody's got to do it. And this next story, as much as it hits close to home, is *definitely* dirty." I turned to camera two. "Two Miami starlets may soon find themselves following in the footsteps of deceased Hollywood actress Mynique Foxx if they don't make some serious changes. Now you may remember Foxx died two weeks ago after an argument with her actor boyfriend turned deadly."

The video from Mynique and Demond's argument outside the MTV party came up on the screen.

"And now," I continued, "two girls who actually are close to me—which is why this story pains me—could be meeting a similar fate."

They pulled up some video from the *Miami Divas* show that showed Sheridan and I out shopping.

"You all know Sheridan Matthews from *Miami Divas* and as the daughter of mega superstar Glenda Matthews. Well, Sheridan is like a sister to me, and that's why I can't stand to see her in a verbally abusive relationship."

It seemed like the studio was silent as the video of Javier talking to Sheridan as if she were a dog, played.

The video stopped and the camera came back to me. "I know some people may say I'm being extreme by saying they'll end up like Mynique, but all it takes is one argument to escalate out of control and lives can be changed forever. Mynique is gone and Demond remains on the run. All in the name of love."

The camera zoomed in. I'd specifically told Manny to do this, even though I knew Dexter was gonna have a fit. "One of the messages I want girls and women to get," I continued, "is that he doesn't have to hit you with his fist. He can hit you with his words and it's just as dangerous." I quickly gave my two cents, then went back to the story before Dexter came racing out of the control room. "But Sheridan is not alone. This guy . . ." I waited as Kendrick's mug shot popped up on the screen. "He's socialite Kennedi Jiles's boyfriend and he's been arrested for domestic abuse before. And now, it seems like he's back to his old ways."

I didn't have video of Kendrick and Kennedi fighting, so I had to tell this story firsthand.

The camera zoomed in on me as I continued. "I saw up close and personal the damage that a guy like Kendrick can inflict on someone. Neither Sheridan nor Kennedi have filed charges. They don't even see anything wrong with their situation. Hopefully, though, this will serve as an eye-opener and they'll take action before they meet a fate like Mynique Foxx. Keep it tuned to *Rumor Central*. We'll be right back after the break."

I had never been so happy to go to commercial. I could only imagine what people were going to think of me, and what my BFFs were going to think of me, but no one had to understand it. If Sheridan and Kennedi weren't my girls, I would've aired the story without a second thought. This was hurting me as much as them. But this was the only way I knew to get through to them. Kennedi's parents would probably nip her relationship in the bud, but I needed to put her on blast because even if they did, she was so strung out behind Kendrick, she'd find a way to keep being with him. Sheridan's mom, even if she did find out about it, would pass the buck off on someone else. But I just wanted to make sure that somebody did something. Even if that meant losing my best friends.

Chapter 28

It was time to face the music, and in this case the music was playing to the tune of two very mad BFFs. I'd purposely kept my phone off all night, hadn't gone on Instagram, and hadn't even checked my email. I'd known that both Sheridan and Kennedi would be calling me and going off, but I needed to give them time to calm down before we could talk. I guess I'd hoped that if they were a little more rational, they'd understand why I had done what I'd done. But judging from the fury on both of their faces as we stood outside of my first-period class, it was obvious there would be no understanding from these two.

"Really, Maya?" Sheridan screamed.

"I can't believe you did that!" Kennedi added.

Sheridan shook her head. "I've seen you sell out some of everybody, but I just never thought you would do it to us. Not like this!"

"Would you two let me explain? Can we go somewhere else and talk about this?" I said, motioning around to the crowd that was starting to gather, several of whom already had popped their phones out, no doubt ready to record and send it to one of the blogs.

"There's nothing you can say that will explain this," Kennedi replied. "I just don't even know what to say. This is a low, even for you."

"Can we just please go in the bathroom and talk?"

Both of them looked around at all the people and thankfully followed me into the girls' bathroom. This girl named Jasmine followed us in as well, but I stopped her at the door. "Excuse me, can we get some privacy?"

"Um, this is a public restroom," she said. "I have to pee."

"Go use the boys'," I replied, as I pushed her out and locked the door.

"Talk," Kennedi said, once I turned back to them. Both of them looked completely disgusted with me. Good thing we weren't fighters, because a different set of friends would be scrappin' right there in the girls' bathroom. "I said, talk," Kennedi repeated when I didn't say anything. "Although I don't know what you think you can say to make this all right."

"I just don't believe you," Sheridan added. "It's one thing to sell out everyone else and to put everyone *else* on blast, but you do *us* like that and we're supposed to be your best friends?"

"Look, let me explain." I let out a heavy sigh. "I just didn't want what happened to Mynique to happen to you guys, too."

"Oh, now you care about Mynique?" Kennedi snapped. "You didn't even like her."

"No, I didn't," I replied. "But I didn't want her dead." I looked at both of them pointedly. "And I don't want either of you dead either."

"Seriously, Maya? Because I had a little fight with my boyfriend, that means I'm going to end up dead?" Kennedi said.

"Any time a man puts his hands on you it's not a *little* fight," I replied. "Demond started fighting with hands. He ended with a gun."

"Kendrick isn't Demond!" she screamed.

"And how did *I* get dragged into this?" Sheridan added. "Javier has never put his hands on me."

"Okay, so you're not being abused physically. But you're verbally and emotionally abused. And that's just as bad," I told her.

"Oh, give me a break," Sheridan said.

"You don't see that what he's doing to you is abuse," I continued. "How he treats you is abusive. Both of you have lost your minds behind these guys and you wouldn't listen to anything I said."

"Oh, and I guess you're the expert on guys," Kennedi said. "Tell me again, what's your boyfriend's name? Oh, that's right, you don't have one."

"That's because she's too busy wrecking everyone else's relationship," Sheridan said, tightening her lips as she glared at me like she hated me.

I knew they were mad, but they weren't even trying to hear my side.

"I just want you to see these guys are no good for you," I told them.

I don't think I'd ever seen Kennedi this angry. "And you think by putting us on Front Street on national TV, that's the way to do it?" Kennedi yelled.

"I tried talking to you," I replied.

"You got all this success and money, but you're just a lonely, jealous gossip girl who gets off by wrecking other people's lives," Sheridan said.

"Why don't you try this novel idea—minding your own business," Kennedi said.

"Oh, she doesn't know how to do that. She's Queen Maya who gets to say and do what she wants," Sheridan added. "She has no business of her own so she has to make her life all about other people's business."

Kennedi started pacing back and forth across the bathroom, almost like she was trying to calm herself down. "My parents didn't see your stupid show, but when they hear about it, they're gonna go ballistic. I swear if they give me a hard time, you are so gonna regret it," Kennedi added.

I had to tell myself that they were angry and therefore give them a pass, but they only had a couple more times with all the threats and degrading comments. "Well, one day you'll thank me for it," I said.

"Oh, so now you're our mamas?" Kennedi snapped, actually stepping in my face.

I didn't back down, even though the fury in her eyes had me a little scared. "Look, I just wanted to do something drastic to give you a wake-up call."

Sheridan nodded as she headed out of the bathroom. "Oh, this was a wake-up call, all right. Come on, Kennedi. She isn't worth it."

Kennedi moved toward the door. "I couldn't agree more. This was a wake-up call to let us know who our friends truly are and aren't." They stopped at the door and stared at me. "And Maya Morgan, you are definitely no longer our friend."

They stormed out, leaving me standing there. I told myself they were just angry. We'd make up.

At least I hoped we would.

Chapter 29

I wanted to cry. And believe me, I didn't cry often. But this was my third time calling both Sheridan and Kennedi and neither one of them would pick up the phone. I'd given them all day to cool off and although neither one of them had had two words to say to me at school, I knew all I had to do was give them time. But, it had been two days now and I was beginning to think they were serious about ending our friendship. Sheridan had unfriended me on Instagram and blocked me on Kik. Kennedi must've blocked my number because every time I tried to call her, I got a message that said, "This phone is not receiving calls." I couldn't believe they were really refusing to talk to me. I couldn't help it. I felt a pain in my heart. I hadn't talked to Alvin since that whole mess with Marisol, and I missed him so much. Shoot, I needed him right about now.

"Forget Marisol," I said, picking up my cell to dial Alvin's number. The phone rang three times, and just when I thought it was about to go to voice mail, someone answered.

"Hello," I said, when no one said anything. "Alvin?" I repeated.

"No, it's not Alvin."

I debated just hanging up but didn't want her to go around wagging her tongue, so I just kind of paused.

"I know this is you, Maya," Marisol snapped. "I see your freakin' name."

"Of course, it's me," I finally said, hating that this chick now knew my number. And I definitely hoped that Alvin had changed how he had me listed in his phone. He had me as *My heart Maya*. We always joked about it, but he wouldn't change it. "Can I speak to Alvin?"

"No, you cannot," she replied.

This chick had definitely gotten a little cocky. The first time I'd met her she'd been like most people, enamored to meet me. But now she was trying to jump bad.

"Girl, put Alvin on the phone. I don't have time to deal with you," I said.

"Look, I tried to play nice with you," she said, trying to sound all tough. "But you need to get your own man and leave mine alone."

"I thought Alvin told you," I said firmly. "We're just friends. Really good friends and it's nothing you can do about that."

"Oh, really," she said. "I've already told him that he needs to end his friendship with you and he agreed."

That caught me off guard. Even though I was mad at Alvin, I couldn't imagine that he would actually kick me to the curb just because his girl said so.

"Why do you think he hasn't talked to you? Why do you think he didn't call you to apologize and clear things up? You know why? Because he promised me," she said, not giving me a chance to answer. "And as you know, Alvin is a good guy. He keeps his promises so he has agreed to stay away from you, because I don't like your relationship."

"Why do you feel threatened by me?" I couldn't help asking.

"I told you, I don't feel threatened by you. I just don't like you. And Alvin's attention needs to be focused on me, not you."

"Put Alvin on the phone," I demanded.

"Obviously," she said, her voice getting louder, "you don't speak English. So, *ese hombre es mi novio, pierde su número.* Lose my man's number." She spoke slowly, as if she wanted to make sure I got it. "Stop hanging on to him. I told him you're not doing anything but leading him on and using him. You don't want him, but you don't want anyone *else* to have him."

I couldn't say anything to that because that was the truth. He had even told me that once before. "Look, I don't have time to deal with you. Just tell Alvin I called."

"No, I will not," she repeated. "As a matter of fact, I'm erasing your number from his phone and don't put him on the spot by making him have to choose, because I guarantee you, sweetheart, he'll choose me."

And before I could say another word, this tramp hung up the phone in my face. I wanted to scream. Not only was I hurt by what she had just said, especially if there was any truth to it (I'd have to catch up with Alvin another time to know for sure), but what was painful for me right now was that I was starting to believe maybe, just maybe, there was some truth to what people were saying. I was losing people I cared about left and right. My cousin Travis was gone, my best friends were gone, and now my best guy friend was gone. Yes, I had a few girls I could call and hang out with, but no one like Sheridan and Kennedi. And definitely no guy like Alvin. I had tried to do the right thing, and now I had never felt so alone.

Chapter 30

So this is what it must feel like to be an outcast. Well, technically, I could never really be an outcast since I still had friends and I was still the It Clique, even if I was the only one in the It Clique, but it felt kind of strange to have my girls completely ignoring me. But that's exactly what Sheridan and Kennedi were doing. What was so tripped out about that was the two of them barely even liked each other but now they were acting like best buds.

"Hi, Maya."

I looked up from my Caesar salad at Nelly Fulton, this girl who had transferred to our school a few months ago. I wanted to ask her why she was even speaking to me, but to be honest I was tired of sitting over here at the lunch table by myself, especially because I could see Shay across the room eating it up. I had plenty of other people I could've sat with, but I wasn't in the mood for anyone asking me a whole bunch of questions about me, Sheridan, and Kennedi.

"Hey, what's going on? Nelly, right?"

She nodded. "Mind if I sit with you?"

I shrugged and motioned toward the seat in front of me.

"So, you're pretty new here, right?" I asked.

"Well, I've been here about a month," she said, sitting down across from me at the cafeteria table.

I shrugged nonchalantly. "So you like it here?" I asked, only because it seemed like the natural question, but honestly I really couldn't care less. I wasn't in the business of making new friends. And yes, this Nelly girl looked like she came from money and had it going on, but right now that's not where my mind was.

"Yeah, I'm liking it a lot," she replied.

"You're a singer, right?" I asked her.

"Yeah, I won *The X Factor*, but my mom insisted that I finish school. Still working on my album and everything."

"Cool," I said. I side-eyed Kennedi and Sheridan, who were sitting across the room laughing like one of them had just told the funniest joke ever. Nelly's eyes made their way over to see what I was looking at.

"Aren't those your friends?" she asked.

"They were." I took a sip of my bottled water. "But whatever." I shrugged, trying to act like it was no big deal. I sat with Nelly and made some more small talk until the bell rang.

The rest of the day was pretty much the same—very few people were speaking to me. That, I was used to. It happened every time a major story broke on *Rumor Central*, but I'd always had Sheridan and Kennedi to have my back. Not anymore.

"All alone, huh?" Bryce, my ex, said, approaching me.

I took a deep breath, folded my arms across my chest, and gave Bryce major attitude.

"And you're talking to me because?"

He tried to smile. "I was just checking on you."

We hadn't really talked since our last breakup. I'd never let on how much that had hurt me, but I definitely wasn't in the mood to deal with him.

"Is there a reason you're invading my personal space?" I

asked him. He'd been waiting outside my fifth-period class like some kind of stalker.

Bryce let out a small laugh. He looked over at Sheridan and Kennedi laughing as they walked down the hall. They didn't even like each other like that. They were just acting like that to get to me.

"Figured you could use a friend."

"Whatever. Go be friends with your busted girlfriend," I mumbled as I walked off. I was so over Bryce, and forget Kennedi and Sheridan, too. If they were going to be mad at me for trying to save them, then whatever, it was their loss.

I made it through the rest of the day without anyone else working my nerve. Right after the dismissal bell rang, I dipped in my fifth-period teacher's room to pick up the instructions for my make-up essay. (It felt like I was forever making up a bad grade.)

After I listened to Ms. Clark's "you can do better" speech, I thanked her, promised to have it in tomorrow, and high-tailed it out of her room. I threw my messenger bag over my shoulder and headed to my car. I had barely rounded the corner when I saw Kennedi and Kendrick going at it. *Why is he always at our school?* My first instinct was to head over there because they looked pretty heated, but I'd done my part. I'd exposed him for the abuser he was, and if Kennedi still chose to stay with him, there was nothing else I could do. I kept it moving, just pretending that I didn't see them.

But I had barely reached the edge of the parking lot when I heard Kendrick shout, "Maya!" I ignored him and kept walking.

"Maya, you hear me!" Kendrick yelled at me again. I could hear his footsteps as he took off in my direction. I looked around to make sure that people were around because if he laid his hands on me, he would definitely be going to jail and I needed witnesses.

"Kendrick, just leave it alone," Kennedi said, coming after him.

She didn't need to worry about protecting me; she needed to worry about protecting herself. I was good. I took my phone out, ready to call 911.

"I just got back in town and saw that mess you did on your show! You think you know everything," he said, stopping in front of me. I just stared at him, still not speaking.

Kennedi pulled on his arm. "Come on, Kendrick. Don't even talk to her. She's a non-factor."

I'll admit that hurt, seeing my friend there, the way she was acting, basically dismissing me.

Kendrick took another step toward me. I pressed the nine and the one on my phone.

"You always up in somebody's business like you know everything," he said, jabbing a finger in my face.

"I know you'd better get your finger out of my face," I calmly said. When he dropped his finger, I continued. "And I know you think it's cool to put your hands on a girl. What's the matter, Kendrick, you can't handle dudes your own size? What was your previous arrest for? Oh, yeah," I said, not waiting for him to answer. "Because you get your jollies by hitting girls."

He glared at me, nothing but hate in his light gray eyes. "That case wasn't what it seemed. I got railroaded."

"Of course you did," I said, turning up my lips.

"You know, while you're trying to put me on blast all on your stupid show, you need to be getting the *real* story."

"Oh, I got the *real* story," I said, waving him off. I dropped my phone back in my purse, since it looked like nothing was about to jump off. Besides, we had enough people standing around watching that if he tried something, I'd be safe.

"Kendrick, leave it alone," Kennedi said again. "Let's just go." She grabbed his arm.

"You're supposed to be the person that we can count on

to bring the truth to the people," he sneered, still glaring at me. "You want to tell everybody's business and you think you're doing your report to make me look bad." He laughed. "But if you gon' tell it, tell it right. It's your girl you need to be doing the report on. She's the psycho abusive one."

Kennedi's lips tightened and her nostrils started flaring. I looked at him, and then back at her.

"B-But I saw bruises," I stammered.

"Yeah, because she was trying to hit me with a friggin' baseball bat and hit her own self in the face."

That was the lamest excuse I ever heard, but the look on Kennedi's face told me he was telling the truth.

"She's the one with the bad temper. She's the one that needs anger management," Kendrick continued.

The fact that Kennedi didn't deny any of what he was saying, made me ask, "What is he talking about, K?" She ignored me and pulled his arm again. He snatched it away.

"Get off of me, Kennedi!" He turned back to me. "Your girl is psychotic. She's violent and she's crazy and the reason I don't want her behind is because I'm going to catch a case messing with her."

Huh? What in the world was he talking about? I had known Kennedi almost her whole life. Yes, she could get really mad, but that was rare and I couldn't believe she'd get so mad as to hit someone. "Kennedi, what is he talking about?" I repeated.

She completely ignored me as she glared at him. "I can't believe you. How are you going to say all that stuff about me?" Kennedi spat at Kendrick.

"Because it's true! You're crazy!" he yelled at her.

This time she actually pushed him. Hard.

"Do you see what I mean?" Kendrick yelled, struggling not to lose his balance. "She's psycho! The bit—"

Saying *that* sent Kennedi over the edge before he could even get the words out. Then, it dawned on me the last time

I had seen her like this was that night at the club when Kendrick was supposed to be out of town and we caught him with Bambi. *She* had been the one smacking him, and he had never hit her back. Was Kendrick right? Was Kennedi the violent one in this relationship?

By the way she was screaming as she pummeled him (I don't know who grabbed her and tried to pull her back but thankfully, someone did), I knew I had this all wrong. The two of them were abusive to each other.

Now, what was I supposed to do?

Chapter 31

I felt like I was in the middle of a really ratchet reality show.

"I told you, I'm sick and tired of you calling me that," Kennedi said, kicking wildly in Kendrick's direction. I was finally able to see that it was one of the teacher's aides (whom no one listened to) trying to pull her off Kendrick.

"You all at this bougie school acting straight hood!" Kendrick shouted. "I might as well be dating a hood rat. I'm sick of you and all this ghetto drama. I keep tryin' to give you chances and you keep tryin' me. So you and your nosey, don't-know-what-she's-talking-about friend can kick rocks!"

"Ghetto! Who are you calling ghetto?" Kennedi screamed more obscenities as she broke from the aide and began clawing for him again. By this time, security started racing over.

Kendrick took off before they reached us, heading to the parking lot, and toward his truck.

"Kennedi, what is wrong with you?" I yelled. She seemed like an out-of-control mad woman.

"Shut up talking to me, Maya! Kendrick!" She took off after him. "You're not leaving! We're not done talking!" she screamed. I followed right behind her because as mad as I

was, I needed to do something before she completely
flipped out.

Kendrick threw open his driver's-side door, jumped inside, started his truck, and took off. Kennedi, tears streaming
down her face, looked around, and before I could say a word,
she snatched my keys out of my hand and took off.

"Have you lost your mind?" I said, taking off after her
again.

Kennedi was running as fast as she could. I was having
trouble keeping up with her, but I caught her on the other
side of the campus parking lot just as she had gotten in my
car and thrown it into reverse. I managed to jump in the passenger side, just as she backed up and sped out of the parking lot.

"Kennedi, what is wrong with you? Have you lost your
freaking mind?" I screamed as she screeched out into the
roadway, barely missing a car.

She pounded the steering wheel as she cried. "He will
not do this to me! He will not do this to me!"

I swear I didn't know what to do or say. It was like my
best friend was possessed. I had never seen anything like it in
my life. "Kennedi, please slow down," I said, thinking that I
needed to try to reason with her because it was obvious that
my friend had flipped out. "Where are you going?"

"I'm just going to get him to talk to me. He just needs to
talk to me," she said, darting in and out of traffic like some
kind of deranged race car driver.

"Kennedi, please slow down, before you get us killed," I
said as I held onto the dashboard.

Kendrick entered onto the freeway, and she turned and
headed right behind him.

"This is all your fault," she snapped.

"How is this *my* fault? All this time I've been talking to

you about him being the violent one. Why didn't you tell me
it was you?"

"Just leave me alone, Maya," she cried.

"Watch out!" I shouted, as a driver blared on his horn
when Kennedi cut his car off.

"He's probably going to that skank's house," she mumbled.

"Since when did you get all worked up behind a guy like
this? Look at what you're doing!" I shouted.

"Just shut up and leave me alone!" she cried, speeding
after him.

Kendrick must've known that we were behind him because he seemed to go faster. Not to be deterred, Kennedi
sped up as well. I looked around in complete fear as I reached
to put my seat belt on. Where was a cop when you needed
one?

"Kennedi, calm down! You're going to kill us. Slow down!
Everybody needs to just cool off and then we can try to talk
to him later." Personally, I hoped he never talked to her again,
but I needed to say anything that would calm her down.

"He's exiting!" she yelled, just as Kendrick made a sharp
right in the middle of the freeway and then, a last-minute exit
to get off, no doubt trying to escape her crazy behind.

Kennedi swerved as well.

"You're going to kill us!" I screamed.

"Ugggghhh!" She let out a piercing scream as several cars
blared their horns. "I'm not letting him do this!"

She took off after him down the exit ramp. "Slow down!"
I yelled.

She swerved again, and then her eyes grew big.

"Kennedi, slow down!" I repeated. We were going down-
hill and had to be doing about eighty miles per hour.

"I—I'm trying!" she said, panicked. I looked down at her
foot pumping the brake. "I'm pressing it and it won't stop!"

"Press harder," I screamed. The car seemed to be going faster and faster. Everything outside was a blur, and then my scream turned into absolute fear as I saw the concrete embankment in front of us—which we were heading directly into. Kennedi swerved. My scream mixed with hers, and there was a loud crash, glass breaking, and then silence as my whole world went black.

Chapter 32

The room felt cold. I couldn't make out where I was. All I knew was that I felt a chill going up my body. It took everything in my power to open my eyes, but I finally managed to flutter them open.

"Mama," I said, trying to make out the figure standing over me.

My mother reached to my side. "Maya, oh, my God! I'm so happy you're awake!" She showered me with kisses all over my face.

I tried to pull myself away from her smothering embrace, but the pain shot up my body, stopping me. "Where am I?" I looked to the side. My dad was on the other side of me. He took both of my hands. Both of my parents looked like they hadn't been to sleep in days. Their eyes were puffy and red.

"Just rest, sweetie," my dad said, stroking my hair.

My hand went up to my forehead and I felt a bandage. "Where am I?" I asked.

"You're in the hospital, sweetie, but you're okay," my mother said. "Thank God, you're okay."

I struggled to get up. "In the hospital for what? What happened?" I felt so groggy it was ridiculous.

"You were in a bad accident," my mother said. "Oh, you had us so scared."

"Accident?" I tried to think. What was the last thing that I remembered? Slowly, it started coming to me. I remembered Kennedi and Kendrick arguing. I remembered him taking off and then we'd jumped in the car and followed him. Kennedi had been driving like a mad woman. And then I'd yelled at her to slow down, but she hadn't.

"Kennedi," I said frantically. "Mom, where's Kennedi?"

"She's okay. You got the brunt of the accident," my mother said. "Kennedi was treated and released."

"How long have I been here?"

"A week," my dad said. "We didn't know . . ." He choked up as his words trailed off and I swear I saw tears in his eyes.

I fell back against the bed and exhaled. Then it dawned on me just how much my entire body ached.

"What's wrong with me?" I asked.

"You had a concussion and some broken bones."

"Broken bones?" My hands immediately went to my face. I hoped my face wasn't scratched up. That was my money-maker.

"You're okay," my mother said, obviously knowing what I was thinking. She stroked my face. "Still beautiful."

I looked toward the hospital room door and noticed Kennedi standing there. Like my parents, her eyes were blood-shot.

"Come on in," my dad said, motioning for her to come over once he noticed her, too.

"This poor child won't leave the hospital. She just sits out there in the lobby, crying," my mom said.

I wondered how much of the real story my parents knew. Would they be inviting her into my room if they knew she was the reason I'd almost died?

Kennedi stood off to the back, apprehensive. I could tell she didn't know what to do or say, and then everything really came back. The argument. The fact that I'd found out *she* was the one who was abusing Kendrick. The fact that her recklessness was why I was here.

Kennedi looked at me and simply said, "Maya, I'm so sorry."

I didn't know what to say. All I could do was turn my head in the opposite direction. My best friend had almost gotten me killed, and behind a guy?

"Maya," she said, taking a step toward me. "Maya, I'm so, so sorry," she repeated.

I had no words for her. She could be sorry all that she wanted. But that wouldn't change a thing. I would never forgive her. As far as I was concerned, she had wanted our friendship to be over, and now it was over.

Chapter 33

The tests for my spinal cord analysis had come back negative, and it looked like as soon as the bumps and bruises healed, I'd be fine. But the doctors said that the healing wouldn't happen overnight.

Unfortunately, that meant I'd be out of pocket for at least two more weeks, which wasn't a good thing. I made a note to try and call Tamara today and see if they could film me from my hospital bed. My mom said Tamara had already called, trying to get the scoop so they could run the story on the show. How they were going to do that in my absence was beyond me because there was nobody who could replace Maya Morgan.

"Knock, knock. Can we come in?"

I rolled my eyes as Kennedi and Sheridan stuck their heads in my door. Kennedi had been here every day for the past four days since I'd been awake, and even though I wouldn't talk to her, she kept coming, talking to me like she hadn't almost killed me.

"Why are you two here?" I said. "Remember, you weren't talking to me." I glared at Kennedi. She looked a mess. Her curly hair was pulled back in a loose ponytail. Her clothes were dirty and wrinkled, like she had been sleeping in them. "Well, that was before you stole my car and tried to kill me," I added.

"We just wanted to check on you," Kennedi said.

"I'm fine, now bye." I turned my head away from them.

"You can be mad at us all you want," Sheridan said, walking over and putting some fresh flowers on the window ledge. "But we're not going anywhere. Just like you wouldn't go anywhere and stay out of our business."

"I don't care what you do," I said. "I dang near died over you and your stupid boy trouble. So do whatever. I'm out of it."

Sheridan and Kennedi exchanged glances. "We just came here to tell you that you were right."

That made me stop and do a double take. "What?"

Kennedi stepped closer to my bed. "Maya, you were so right. The last week and a half has been the scariest of my life. To think you could've died over me running behind some guy is killing me." Her eyes watered up as she continued. "I loved him to the point that it was obsessive."

"Ya think?" I said, raising an eyebrow at her as I shifted in my bed.

She continued. "I don't know what it is about Kendrick that pushed all my buttons, that, shoot, pushed me over the edge, but I had to take a good long look at myself. That wasn't me."

I just stared at her because if she wanted me to come to her defense, it wasn't about to happen.

"My point is," she continued. "You know how I felt about saving myself for the right guy. And I guess the fact that I thought he was the right one and then he turned out to be a jerk caused me to flip and if I'm being honest, I probably pushed him away by acting so crazy."

Sheridan stepped up to Kennedi's side. "We both kinda lost ourselves with our guys," she added.

I didn't know what had happened to make her have a change of heart, especially since she'd been so adamant that Javier was a good guy.

"I just wanted someone to love me," she said.

"What you guys had wasn't love," I couldn't help but say.

I expected her to roll her eyes or go off. I was shocked when she said, "I know. I just didn't want you to be right about Javier. I didn't want to admit how stupid I'd been behind him." She sighed heavily. "He ran up one of my credit cards and stole my phone."

"What?"

"Stole it right out of my purse, although he claimed he didn't take it. I let him use my card because he claimed he had to buy something for his mom. Yeah, he bought something all right, a big-screen TV, and a whole bunch of other stuff."

All I could do was shake my head. A lot had happened since I'd been in the hospital.

"When I called him on it"—she looked down at the floor—"he went off on me. He called me every degrading name in the book and as he was going left, I just heard your voice, telling me I deserved better." She forced a smile. "I do deserve better. We're saying all that to say that we are so sorry that we didn't listen."

"And I'm so sorry that I caused you to be here," Kennedi said, tears welling in her eyes.

I probably should've said that it wasn't her fault, but it was, so I kept my mouth closed. She was lucky that the doctor said I'd be all right once I healed because I didn't know that we could've repaired our relationship if the situation had been different.

Shoot, I still didn't know if we could repair it. We'd been through a lot.

"So, they say my car is totaled," I said, wanting to change the subject. I missed my friends, but I didn't know that I was ready to forgive them.

Surprisingly, my dad hadn't even been mad when he'd told me about my car. I guess he really was just happy that I was alive.

Kennedi slowly nodded. "But my parents are going to pay for everything."

I rolled my eyes. That was the least of my concerns. "What happened? Why didn't you stop?" I asked her.

Kennedi hunched her shoulders. "I mean, I know I was driving crazily, but you know I'm a good driver. It's like I couldn't stop. Like the brakes just wouldn't work."

"Yeah, that's a top-of-the-line BMW," I said. "My brakes aren't just gonna stop working." I know I sounded a little bitter and I wasn't cutting her any slack, but she wasn't the one laid up in a hospital bed with tubes sticking out of every part of her body.

"I just don't understand how this accident happened," Sheridan said.

"Because Kennedi was driving like Batman, that's how."

Kennedi lowered her head in shame.

"No, that might not be the case."

All three of us turned toward the tall man with a head full of gray hair and a cheap-looking suit who had just stepped into my hospital room.

"May I help you?" I said.

"Yes, I'm Detective Paul Yukon," he said, easing into the room. "May I come in? I just wanted to talk to you for a bit."

"Talk to me about what?" I said. I knew I probably should've called my parents and gotten their permission or something, but I didn't understand why the police would be in my room.

"Well, I'm investigating your accident," he said, walking over to my bed. "You are Maya Morgan, right?"

I nodded. "But why would my accident need investigating? I mean, it was a single car wreck."

The detective looked down at his notepad. "Were you driving a silver BMW?"

"*I* wasn't," I said. "She was." I pointed at Kennedi. Yes, I was going to rat her out if I had to.

"Well, we got a tip that someone was seen tampering with your vehicle prior to the accident."

"Tampering?" I said, shocked.

Kennedi and Sheridan looked confused as well.

"Upon further investigation," the detective continued, "we found that your brake line had been cut."

I sat straight up in my bed, and immediately grimaced from the pain that shot up my back. I shook it off. "Brake line cut? What are you talking about?"

The detective walked over closer to my bed. "We pulled the school surveillance video. He reached in his pocket and pulled out his phone, swiped the screen, then held the phone out to me.

"Press play," he said.

I did and video of a burgundy Honda Accord pulling into the parking lot popped up on the screen. The driver pulled up behind my parked car, jumped out, and disappeared on the side of the vehicle. I couldn't tell if the person was a man or a woman. He or she was dressed in a dark, oversized hoodie and some baggy jeans. The timestamp on the video said 1:19 PM. The middle of the school day.

"How do you know they're messing with my car?" I asked after the video stopped. The person had disappeared on the side of my car and you couldn't see anything that was going on.

"We don't." He took the phone back and dropped it in his pocket. "We got a tip from someone who thought they'd seen someone tampering with your car. So, we checked your car out at the impound. The brakes had been cut. Now, we're just following up all leads. Do you recognize the car or the driver?"

I shook my head. "I have no idea who that is. And I've never seen that car before."

He handed me a business card. "If you can think of any-thing or anyone who would want to do you harm, please give me a call."

Anyone who wanted to do me harm? Shoot, where in the world would I begin in making that long list?

Chapter 34

Somebody had tried to kill me.

Somebody really and truly had tried to kill me. The detective's words were swirling in my head. It wasn't Kennedi who almost killed me. It was some deranged person who wanted me dead.

"I don't understand," I told the officer after I took his card. I couldn't let him go without getting some more information.

Detective Yukon replayed the scenario several times. He said their investigation was in the early stages, but they believed the reason Kennedi hadn't been able to stop was because the brake line had been tampered with just enough so it wouldn't fail until my car hit a high rate of speed. I guess whoever wanted me to crash wanted it to happen in the worst possible way.

"So," the detective said, closing up his notepad. "Do you have any idea who would want you dead?"

"Wow," I said. "I mean, I know a lot of people that want me fired or can't stand me, but dead?"

My mind immediately raced to Demond Cash. He'd threatened me, told me I would be sorry. Or maybe it was Kendrick. Kennedi said she hadn't heard from him since the accident. Maybe that's what he had been doing on campus in the first place. But then he had been driving his Escalade.

"Did you run the plates?" I asked.

"Couldn't get a good read off the security camera, but we're working on it."

"Are you sure this wasn't an accident?" I side-eyed Kennedi. "She *was* driving crazy."

"Well, that's what we believed at first," Detective Yukon said. "But even though those brakes were cut haphazardly, meaning it wasn't a professional job, it was definitely someone who knew what they were doing. And someone who wanted to hurt you. Bad."

"Demond Cash." I said the name out loud. "That's the only person I could think who would want me dead. He said I ruined his life and that I would pay."

The detective opened his notepad back up and scribbled on it. "Demond Cash. Where have I heard that name before?"

"The actor Demond Cash," I said.

The detective stopped writing and stared at me. "Wow, okay."

"I did a story on him and his girlfriend, and he wasn't too happy about it."

"You'll have to excuse me—I don't watch much TV," the officer said. "Nor am I hip to all the latest Hollywood happenings."

"Well, that needs to be where you start because if anybody wanted me dead, it was him. He's reportedly on the run, wanted in connection with the murder of his girlfriend," I added.

"Okay, we'll definitely look into that," the officer said, scribbling some more on his notepad. "Well, the doctor said I shouldn't stay in here long." He headed toward the door. "Again, call me if you think of anything. You continue recovering, and I hope that I'll have some news for you soon."

"Wow, you made the wrong person mad this time," Sheridan said once he'd left the room. She stopped talking and looked like she was thinking. "Wait a minute. Javier has a burgundy Honda Accord. I mean, it hasn't been working," she said. "But maybe he got it fixed."

"Javier? You think he had something to do with this?"

Sheridan shrugged. "I don't know. When I broke it off with him, he swore that you had been in my ear. I tried to tell him that you didn't even know about it."

"And you think he'd try to kill me over that?" I said.

"I mean, I don't think so, but I don't know," she said.

"Well, you need to go catch that detective and give him Javier's name, too," I told her, pointing toward the door.

Sheridan looked hesitant.

"Really, Sheridan?"

"No, no. You're right. I'll be right back," she said, turning and scurrying out of the room.

Kennedi and I sat in silence for a minute.

"I'm so sorry, Maya."

"Yeah, you already said that." I couldn't help it—I couldn't stay mad at Kennedi. "But if what that detective said was true, then what happened wasn't really your fault. Whoever had it out for me would've gotten me eventually anyway."

I was stunned. It was one thing to be disliked. Or even for someone to wish me harm. But for someone to actually try to kill me—that was my wake-up call.

Chapter 35

I was so ready to get out of this hospital, I thought I was going to scream. It had been two weeks since the accident, and I felt much better, to the point that they were letting me leave earlier than I'd originally thought. Unfortunately, my doctor had no faith in my ability to take it easy, as he said. So he wouldn't let me leave until tomorrow. Personally, I think my mother had something to do with it. She knew I was determined to find out who was behind running me off the road and the only way she could keep an eye on me was to keep me locked down in this hospital room.

J. Love had come by yesterday. He was the reason my room was filled with all kind of fresh flowers. Alvin had been by, as well. Apparently, all that mess Marisol was talking about him staying away from me was a lie because he had no idea what I was talking about when I asked him about it. Even my ex, Bryce had dropped in. It did feel good to know that there were so many people that cared about me. My nurse, a nice elderly woman who reminded me of my grandmother, called me a player because of the "men I had traipsing in and out." I'd laughed and told her those were nothing but boys, hence the reason I was single.

"So, what did you find out?" I asked Tamara.

Tamara had just hung up her cell phone. She had been working to try to help me get to the bottom of who messed with my brakes. Of course, I knew she was doing it for ratings, but whatever.

"We're on it," she said. "Police still have no leads, but they're hoping that with our story we'll get someone to call in."

"So, when do you want me to come in and do the story?"

"Yeah, um, about that . . ." she said uneasily.

That made me sit straight up in my bed. Tamara had delivered enough bad news in the two years I'd been working for her for me to know when it was coming. "Yes?"

"Well, the doctor is not clearing you to return to work."

"I get out of here tomorrow," I said.

"Yeah, but your mom gave me permission to talk to your doctor, and he said you won't be cleared for work for an additional two weeks."

"What?" I said. "That's ridiculous!"

"Well, you're going to have to take that up with him, but in the meantime *Rumor Central* cannot continue to wait. We've already been off air two weeks."

"So, what does that mean?"

"Well, we have someone that's going to fill in," she said.

"Fill in?" We'd been down that road before. No one could replace me on *Rumor Central*. They'd tried to give another show to Evian, my former *Miami Divas* costar. That idea had backfired. I thought they'd come to their senses and seen that there was only one Maya Morgan.

Tamara must've read my mind, because she said, "Look, nobody's looking to replace you, but this is business. We have to keep the show going. We're about to hit Oscar season and the spring slew of movies, and we can't afford to be on hiatus."

"I can do it," I protested.

"And we can't be responsible should you come to work and pass out or something. Or worse, re-injure yourself."

"I'm not going to sue you guys. I'll sign a waiver or anything."

Tamara shook her head like it was a done deal. "Maya, it's just a couple of weeks. It's just three shows."

"Three shows?" I said. "You said the doctor only had me out for two weeks."

"Well." She shifted again nervously. "We're taping one this evening."

My mouth fell open. "Taping with whom?" I asked.

"It's a young girl. She actually goes to your school, so we're going to keep it all in the family." She smiled like she was doing me a favor. "This g—"

"Who?" I screamed, cutting her off.

"Her name is Nelly Fulton. She's the winner of *The X Factor*. She comes with a huge fan base."

I didn't care if she came with Oprah as her number-one fan. I didn't want her filling in on my job.

"Look, I have to go," Tamara said, throwing her purse over her shoulder. "It's a done deal. Nelly is just filling in until you come back."

"How did Nelly get my job?"

"She does not have your job," Tamara said, heading toward the door. "Calm down and stop being dramatic. She's just holding it down until you get back. Your fans are calling in wanting to know what happened. We've run a story on the news, but we've got to get *Rumor Central* up and on the air." She smiled. "So make sure you tune in today at five." And with that, she flashed a smile and walked out the door.

As soon as the door closed. I let out a piercing scream and threw a glass, causing it to shatter. If Tamara heard it, she didn't care because nothing but silence filled the room after that.

Chapter 36

This could not be happening. I sat straight up in my bed hoping that this was just a cruel trick Tamara was playing on me. But since I was in the hospital room and I doubted they could tap into the hospital television system, I was all too sure that the theme music playing on my TV, *my* theme music, was all too real.

"What's up, everybody, it's your girl Nelly Fulton, filling in for Maya Morgan on *Rumor Central*, and you know I've got the scoop."

This heffa couldn't even be original. She was using my lines word for word. I couldn't hear much of what she said after that, though, because my ears were burning with rage. This was *my* show. I understand that the show had to go on, but they could've come and filmed me from my hospital bed. Shoot, they could've released me, let me go film, and then sent me back home. What they *didn't* need to do was give anybody the idea that they could take my job. And I don't care about any reassurances that Tamara tried to give me. There was always a possibility that they could have a serious brain lapse and give someone else my job permanently, because Lord knows somebody was always jockeying for it.

"I need to take your blood pressure," the small, meek nurse said, walking in.

"Can you come back?" I snapped.

"Excuse me?"

"I need to be alone, okay? Can you just come back?"

The nurse looked like she wanted to say something to me, but decided against it. "Fine, I'll be back in ten minutes."

I didn't say anything as I continued staring at the TV screen. They had a picture of me and then damage from the wreckage as Nelly ran down the story and how police were searching for the person who cut my brakes.

Nelly wrapped up my story, and I hit the mute button on the TV and tossed the remote across my bed.

"Ugh!" I screamed. I didn't know how long I sat there seething before the nurse stuck her head back in my hospital room.

"Can I come in now?"

"Fine," I said, shrugging.

"You really shouldn't let stuff get you so upset," she said as she took a device and wrapped it around my arm.

"You really should mind your own business," I replied.

She giggled and mumbled. "Well, isn't that the pot calling the kettle black?"

"Excuse me?" I said.

"Nothing, Miss Morgan, nothing at all."

The nurse pumped the little contraption in her hand and then turned to me. "Do you need any pain meds?"

"No," I grumbled. "I just need to be left alone."

She fumbled around with the machine some more as *Rumor Central* came back on. I almost turned the TV off and in fact, had just reached for the remote when the picture on the screen caught my eye. I hit the mute button to unmute it just as Nelly said, "And so police say Javier Espinosa was alone at the time of the robbery."

"Robbery?" I said. Good grief! My friends' taste in guys

was just un-freaking-believable. Sheridan said he'd stolen from her, but robbery?

"Authorities say he used the cell phone of former *Miami Diva* Sheridan Matthews, his girlfriend, to pose as her assistant in order to set up meetings with celebrities. Espinosa had the celebrities meet him, at which time he'd rob them at gunpoint."

"Can you please be still?" the nurse asked.

I jerked my hand away from her and gave her the finger to be quiet. "Oh, my God," I said. My friends were going to learn to listen to me yet. Too bad for them they had learned the hard way.

Chapter 37

To say I was in a foul mood would be the understatement of the year. I was livid, not just about the *Rumor Central* report, but because once again, my dad had had something too important come up and he was going to try to leave me in this hospital another few hours. My mom also couldn't get away until later this afternoon. Yeah, I know I wasn't scheduled to leave until one and it was only ten, but the doctor said I could go and I was ready to go! And they expected me to just wait here until they made time? Oh, I didn't think so.

"Are you sure you can leave?" Alvin asked, as he got the last of the flowers out my room.

"My papers are signed and ready for me to go," I said, slipping my jacket on. I flinched from the pain, but it was nowhere near as bad as it had been a couple of days ago. I was just going to plaster on a smile and keep it moving because the last thing I wanted was to have the doctor try to make me wait on my family.

"It's just a couple hours, Maya. You don't think you should just chill?" Alvin asked.

"Look, I didn't call you to come and get me for a lecture, okay?" I snapped.

"Why are you in such a bad mood?" he asked. Then he stopped and studied me. "This is because of Nelly doing your show yesterday, huh?"

I actually felt tears welling up in my eyes, not just because my anger about everything was coming to a head, but because Alvin really was the only one who got me. No one else had been able to tell just how much having Nelly replace me hurt. But I hadn't said a word to Alvin about it and he'd known when I'd first called him. I could hear it in his voice when he'd asked me was I okay. He'd been at the hospital every day since my accident. My mom had said on the first day he'd slept in the waiting room. Alvin was a good guy. I wished I could've been the girl that he wanted me to be.

"I'll get over it," I finally told him. It was too late to be pining over Alvin now. He may not admit it, but Marisol had made it clear, they were boyfriend and girlfriend now. "I just want to get home."

"Come on, I'll take you home. Your parents can meet you there and I'm going to stay with you and we're going to watch movies all day long." I smiled as he helped me stand up off the hospital bed.

"Wait! Wait!" the nurse said, coming in. "That's my job."

"No," Alvin said, smiling at her. "That's my job."

I managed to return his smile as he helped me into the stupid wheelchair that they said was mandatory that I leave in.

The nurse looked at the papers in her hand. "Okay, fine. I'd still feel better if your parents were here, but they did sign the discharge papers."

"Which means I'm free to go," I said, motioning for Alvin to move toward the door.

One day I'd come back and thank the doctor who'd helped me and the few nurses who I liked, but for now, I wanted to get the heck up outta here.

Alvin got me situated and in his car, and on the ride

home, he asked, "Do you want to get something to eat? Maybe a big, fat calorie-laden burger?"

I smiled. Normally I wouldn't be caught dead eating anything like that, but after weeks of hospital food, that was just what the doctor ordered.

"Yeah," I told him. "I'd love that."

Fifteen minutes later, he pulled up in Smashburger, ordered us both burgers and fries to go, and then continued on to my house.

At home, Alvin got me settled, treating me like a queen, refusing to let me do anything for myself. I actually enjoyed the attention and the pampering almost as much as he enjoyed giving it.

"So, any leads?" he said, once we had finished eating our burgers and were sitting on the sofa.

"No, they can't seem to trace the burgundy Honda Accord. The camera didn't get a good view of the plate."

Alvin sat straight up. "Burgundy Honda Accord?"

I stretched, feeling belly-fat full and suddenly gross from that burger. "Yeah, whoever messed with my brakes was driving a burgundy Honda Accord. I thought I told you that."

"No, you didn't," he said in shock. He looked like he was thinking. "Wait a minute. When did this happen?"

I looked at him, confused. "What do you mean, when did this happen? You know when it happened."

He hesitated, still thinking. Finally, his mouth dropped open. "Oh, my God."

"What, Alvin? What?" The look on his face was scaring me.

"It—it can't be."

"What can't be, Alvin?" I repeated. "What are you talking about?"

"The day of your accident. I haven't told you, but I broke it off with Marisol. For good."

"What?" I said. He looked directly at me. "I told her I was in love with you and that she and I had no future. And it wasn't fair for me to keep seeing her."

"In love with me," I said, staring him straight in the eye. I knew how much he cared about and liked me. But love?

"Yes, Maya, you know that," Alvin said. "You know that I love you. But"—he shook himself out of a trance he seemed to be going into—"but my point is, Marisol was livid and she kept mumbling how you ruined everything for her."

"Okay, so she didn't like me, but what does that have to do with the person who was trying to kill me?"

He turned to me. "Maya, Marisol has been driving her brother's car. It's a burgundy Honda Accord."

Chapter 38

I'd known that Marisol hated me. I'd just had no idea how much. But now, everything was making perfect sense. Now I understood why someone would want me dead. She wanted me out of the picture. It didn't have anything to do with *Rumor Central* or Demond Cash. It was all Marisol. She wanted her life with Alvin so bad that she was willing to try and get it by any means necessary. And if that meant killing me, then that was exactly what she would do.

"Are you sure you want to be here?" Alvin said.

We were inside his house in his living room. This was one of the rare times that his mother was out of town. She'd gone on a gambling trip with one of her friends. Alvin had been super upset when he'd put all the pieces together and discovered it was Marisol behind my accident, but when we'd taken that information to the police, they'd given the typical "we'll investigate," but he wasn't about to sit around and wait on that, especially when the sergeant had told Alvin a confession would make this an open-and-shut case. Alvin was determined after that.

"I'm okay with being here," I said. "Are you sure you want to do this?"

Now, I definitely wanted to catch Marisol, but Alvin was
my boy and I didn't want him to do anything that would
bother his conscience later. He was one of the good guys, and
I knew he actually cared about Marisol, although he tried to
downplay it now, so this couldn't be easy. Alvin used his hand
to gently move a piece of hair that had fallen in my face.

"She messed with my Maya. Nobody messes with my
Maya," he said.

His Maya. That made me smile.

We heard a car door slam outside and Alvin said, "She's
here. So you got the camera set up?"

I nodded, looking around at the three hidden cameras
that our photographer had placed strategically throughout
the home.

"You need to keep it under wraps, okay? I got this." He
shot me a warning look.

"Why? What are you talking about?" I said, trying to
feign confusion.

"You. You let me handle this. Stay in your hiding place,"
he said, motioning toward the closet. He'd planned to sit on
the sofa, where I could get a good view from the side of the
closet. The only way Alvin would agree to my being here was
if I hid. I'd wanted to sit front and center, but Alvin was right.
There was no way we'd get a confession if she saw me.

"I'll behave," I said. He gently kissed me on the cheek just
as the doorbell rang. I squeezed his hand for reassurance and
then darted to my hiding place in the closet.

"Hey, Marisol," he said, opening the door. She was grinning from ear to ear.

"Hey, handsome."

"Come on in."

She smiled as she sashayed in, decked out in her Sunday
best. She had on an outfit that said, *I'm going to catch my man.*

Just enough makeup to turn Alvin on, but not so much it would turn him off.

"So, I'm so glad you called me," she said, dropping her purse and sitting in the recliner, where neither I nor the camera could get a good look. *No, no,* I thought. She needed to move so that the camera could hit her face on.

Alvin walked over, reached his hand out to her, and pulled her up from the seat. He took her into a big bear hug, which seemed to catch her by surprise because she said, "Wow, I wasn't expecting that."

"Just seeing you, I just wanted to hug you," he casually said.

I couldn't help it. I knew we were on a mission, but that made me cringe.

"So, what's going on?" Marisol said. "You said you wanted to talk to me about our relationship."

He took her hand and led her to the sofa, and I couldn't help but smile. Perfect. That shot would be perfect.

"I just—I just wanted to apologize for the way that everything went down," Alvin began. "I know I hurt you."

She lost her smile. "Yeah, you hurt me really bad, Alvin."

"I wasn't trying to," he said. "I've tried to be honest with you from the very beginning. I told you how I felt about Maya."

"Yeah," Marisol said. "But you also told me that she didn't return your feelings."

He nodded. "I know that, but the heart wants what it wants."

She stopped and stared at him. "So I guess your heart didn't want me."

He squeezed her hand. "It's not that, Marisol. You are beautiful, smart—"

She jerked her hand away. "But I'm not some nosey, gossipy tramp."

It took everything in my power not to bounce from that closet, but I continued waiting.

"She's not a tramp."

"See, this is what I'm talking about!" Marisol snapped. "You're always defending her. You're supposed to be my man, but you're defending her."

"But that's just it, Marisol." Alvin sighed. "I never agreed to be your man. I simply told you that I wasn't seeing anyone else."

"And neither was I, so that meant we were exclusive," she said.

"I was trying to be fair to you."

"Being fair to me is giving me a shot. But you could never give me a shot because of her. She doesn't deserve you. If only she . . ."

"Come on, come on, come on," I muttered quietly.

"If only she what?" Alvin asked.

She bit down on her lip, took a deep breath, then defiantly said, "If only she wasn't in the picture."

"But she is," Alvin said.

"I don't know how," she mumbled.

"What is that supposed to mean?" he asked.

"Nothing," she said as she stood up and began pacing.

"Sit down," I mumbled from the closet. "Sit down so the camera can get you."

"Can you come sit back down so we can talk?" Alvin asked.

She looked like she was debating it and then, finally, stomped over and sat back down next to him.

"All I'm saying is, she isn't that bad and I don't understand what you meant by 'if she wasn't in the picture' because she is. As a matter of fact, she came home from the hospital today."

"What?" she said. I had never seen anyone look so disappointed. "Are you freaking kidding me? She's fine?"

Alvin looked at her. "Yeah, why wouldn't she be?"

"Because I—" Marisol stopped talking.

"What did you do?" Alvin asked.

"Nothing." She clamped her lips shut.

"Tell me the truth, Marisol." He lowered his voice and gently said, "The whole reason that I called you over here is to tell you that I know there's no hope for Maya and I, and the thought of losing you makes me know more than ever that you're the one I want."

"Really?" she said.

"Yes."

I couldn't help but narrow my eyes. Alvin was laying it on thick. I hadn't known he was capable of lying like that. I shook it off. He was acting, not lying.

"But I need to know the truth," he continued. "Because that means a lot to me that you would go to such lengths so we could be together."

She smiled as she stroked his face. "Alvin, you just don't know. I would do anything so that we could be together."

"Does that mean getting rid of Maya?"

"Anything," she repeated.

"So, what did you do? Did you cut her brakes?" Alvin forced a smile when she didn't answer. "You *did*. You cut her brakes. Wow, you really would go to any length. You just don't know what that means."

"Really?" she asked. "You're not mad?"

He shook his head like he was in shock.

"Say it, say it," I said, muttering the words from in the closet. I needed the words to come out of her mouth. I hoped Alvin realized that she still hadn't officially confessed.

"How did you know how to cut brakes? Dang, girl, you're talented." He actually looked proud.

"I didn't work in my brother's auto repair shop for nothing," she proudly said. It was like she was relaying how she discovered a cure for cancer or something. "You have to do it just enough where it won't give until she reaches a certain speed, then when she tries to stop, the brakes go out. It's really not that hard."

"Wow," he said. "But she could've been killed."

"And?" Marisol shrugged. "She wasn't," she added, disappointed. "She's like a freaking cockroach. You try to stomp her and stomp her, and she still won't die."

Oh, I'd had enough. Alvin was just going to have to be mad. I bounced out of that closet.

"I got your cockroach!" I screamed. "And I'm sure you're going to see plenty of them, when they put you under the jail!"

Marisol looked shocked as she jumped up, looked at me, then back at Alvin. "What's going on?" she asked him. I could see fear creep up in her eyes. She was cold busted and she knew it.

"Marisol, I can't believe you," Alvin said. He looked at her, his eyes full of pain.

"Can't believe what?" So, she really was going to try and play dumb?

"So you thought, what?" Alvin said and I could tell he was getting angrier and angrier. "You thought you could just off Maya and everything between me and you would be fine? You thought you could kill her and we'd be together?"

Marisol looked like she was trying to come up with a good explanation. Finally, she said, "I can't stand her!" She turned to me and the hate in her eyes was unbelievable. "Why do you get everything? The dream job, the money, and the guy? Why couldn't you have died?"

Before I knew anything, Marisol was on me, screaming as she wrapped both hands around my neck.

"Die! Why couldn't you just die?"

I clawed at her hands, as I tried to get a scream out. Alvin was trying to pull her off me, but she was like a mad woman. He did manage to loosen her grip and I could breathe.

"Get off me," I screamed, scrambling away. "Help!"

By that point, Alvin managed to pull her into a bear hug. I went straight for my phone and called 911. And I didn't breathe easy until ten minutes later, when police had her in handcuffs and were carting her off to jail.

Chapter 39

I hadn't had a slumber party since I was thirteen years old. But we were more than making up for it tonight. Just the three of us—me, Sheridan, and Kennedi. Their little fake, let's-make-Maya-mad closeness had actually morphed into a real closeness. They were no longer making snide comments at one another and doing eye rolls, and their friendship really seemed genuine. It actually made me very happy. I had been trying to get the two of them to click for years. I hated that it had taken our friendship dang near being destroyed, but they'd finally clicked.

So, I was one happy diva.

Marisol was behind bars, and probably would be for a good minute. She'd tried to wrestle the police officer's gun from him at the station, so she'd added an additional charge of assault on a police officer.

I was back at work. Although Nelly was hanging around a lot more than I would've liked, they hadn't given her my job.

Aunt Bev was doing better, and even though Travis was staying in Brooklyn, we FaceTimed each other on a regular basis.

And now I was chilling with my girls, doing what we did best, hanging out and talking about boys.

"OMG, that is hilarious. I can't believe Roscoe Bailey is looking for Javier," I said, referring to this hip hop record producer that was known for his thuggish ways. Sheridan had just filled us in on the latest. Javier had made bail, but apparently, he'd hightailed it out of town once he'd heard who was after him.

"Yes," Sheridan replied. "You remember Kayla?"

"I forgot that was Roscoe's niece," I said.

"Yep. Well, she's one of the people Javier got out my phone and robbed. He actually stole a gold necklace Roscoe had gotten for her."

"Wow. He'd better hope that the police get him before Roscoe does," I said.

Sheridan threw her arms up. "I don't know and I don't care."

I needed to keep our conversation light because the last thing I wanted was this night to go south. But I really was glad to see that Sheridan had come to her senses about him. A part of me was glad that he'd stolen from her, if that's what it had taken to open her eyes.

Kennedi, on the other hand, was not as strong. I could still see the pain in her eyes behind Kendrick. As part of the therapy that her mother made her attend once the whole story came out, she opened up about how empty she felt without him. Kennedi had come to terms with her obsessive behavior with Kendrick, or at least she'd told the therapist that she'd come to terms. Granted, it had only been three weeks, and I knew that Kennedi getting over Kendrick would be a long work in progress.

I've learned that Alvin was right about one thing—sometimes you have to let those you love make and learn from their own mistakes. Although my heart was in the right place, maybe I did push too hard.

"I heard Kendrick was dating Bambi," Kennedi said out of the blue.

I didn't want her getting all sad again, so I said, "Well, if he could move on from all that fabulosity"—I motioned up and down her body—"to that ghetto reject chick, then you didn't need him."

Kennedi gave a half smile. "I know you're right. But I still love him."

"Ugh," I groaned before I realized it.

Luckily, she laughed. "Nah, I'm good. I love him. But this wise young woman once told me that I need to love myself more."

I smiled at that, but didn't say anything about it. "Get your drinks." We held up our cans of Sprite.

"To us. And our renewed motto of 'BFF before boys,' " Sheridan said.

Then, we heard a voice say, "Does that include men, too?"

I turned to see Alvin standing in the door to my bedroom. "What are you doing here?" I said, jumping up off my bed and racing over to him. I hugged him tight. I still felt a little soreness, but it was nothing major.

"Your mom let me up. She told me you were up here holding a party." Alvin looked great in a purple and gold Polo shirt and some baggy jeans. He still wore those nerd glasses, but he'd definitely upgraded his game.

"Wow," Sheridan said, "your mom lets boys come up to your room?"

I turned to face her. "Girl, please. You got me twisted. I do what I want to do," I replied.

"And what you must want to do is go live on the streets." My mom appeared right on the side of Alvin, giving me the side eye. "I knew it was three of you. Besides, I like Alvin." She pushed the door open. "But keep this door wide open."

Sheridan and Kennedi burst out laughing as my mother walked on down the hall.

"Busted," Sheridan said.

We laughed as Alvin held out a pizza box. "I figured you ladies would be hungry. So, I brought you a vegetarian pizza."

"Ugh," Kennedi said, staring in the box. "Why someone would eat a pizza with vegetables makes no sense."

I reached in the box and took a slice, as did Sheridan. "That's because you can eat a triple meat pizza and not gain a pound." I took a bite and savored the slice of pizza.

"Thanks, Alvin," Sheridan said.

"Yeah, thanks, Alvin," I added.

"You know it was my pleasure." We stood there for a minute, staring at each other.

"Do you, um—do you want to stay?" I finally asked.

"What?" Kennedi and Sheridan said at the same time.

"I know it's girls' night," Alvin replied, smiling. "Plus, I'm sure your mom gave me a time limit on how long I can be up here."

"I did!" my mom yelled from down the hall. I wanted to die of embarrassment, but Alvin just laughed.

"Let me walk you down," I told him.

He waved good-bye to Kennedi and Sheridan as we walked downstairs. I felt flutters in my stomach as we made our way to the front door. But this time, I didn't try and fool myself about what they were. I knew. I liked Alvin. A lot.

And I thought it was time that I took him up on his offer and gave him a chance.

He stood at my front door. For a minute, I thought he would try to kiss me, but then, just as he was about to lean in, his eyes made their way over my shoulder and he stood up straight. "Bye, Mrs. Morgan. Enjoy your evening."

I turned to see my mom standing behind me, grinning like crazy.

"Mom!" I said.

She just giggled, waved, and then scurried into the kitchen.

"Call me later, okay?" Alvin said. "After everyone goes to bed. I want to hear your voice before you go to sleep."

I paused. "I will because, um, ah, I have something important I want to talk to you about."

He nodded. I wondered if he had any idea I was about to tell him I wanted to be his girl. "I can't wait," he said.

I smiled as I shut the door. Once I got back upstairs, Kennedi and Sheridan were waiting for me.

"Ummmph, 'BFF before boys,' huh?" Sheridan said.

"I'm back, aren't I?" I said, laughing.

"Yeah, but you were ready to sell us out in a minute," Kennedi said.

"But Alvin is a good one. So, for him, we'll take a back seat," Sheridan added. "Just not tonight."

"That's right," I said. "Tonight it's no boys."

"And no boy trouble," Kennedi added.

Sheridan chimed in, "Tonight is all about us."

Then, we all said it together, "It's all about BFFs before boys!"

Then we turned up the music and danced the night away.

Domestic Violence is real

If you or someone you know is in an abusive relationship,
please call 1-866-331-9474 or visit

www.loveisrespect.org

#lovedoesnthurt

BOY TROUBLE

ReShonda Tate Billingsley

ABOUT THIS GUIDE

The following questions are intended to
enhance your group's reading of
BOY TROUBLE.

DISCUSSION QUESTIONS

1. Initially, Maya decided not to run the video of Mynique and Demond fighting outside of the club. Why do you think she didn't? Why do you think she eventually decided to show it?

2. One of the things everyone kept telling Maya was that she needed to mind her own business. Should she have done that, or was she right to be concerned? Where should she have drawn the line?

3. Why do you think Maya was so concerned with her friends' relationships? Do you think she would've been as concerned if she'd had her own relationship?

4. Sheridan never saw her relationship as being abusive. Why do you think she ignored the signs?

5. Kendrick seemed to bring out the worst in Kennedi. Do you agree that she was obsessive behind him?

6. Why do you think Kennedi never told Maya that she was the abusive one in the relationship?

7. Maya forgave Kennedi for the accident that could've killed her. Do you think she was right to forgive her?

8. Why do you think Maya was so worried about having someone fill in for her on *Rumor Central*?

9. Although Marisol went too far in her anger at Maya, do you think she was right to be upset with Maya? What could Alvin have done differently?

10. Why do you think Maya finally decided to give Alvin a chance?

Next in the Rumor Central series

Eye Candy

Chapter 1

I needed my own page in Webster's Dictionary. That's because, if you looked up the word *fabulous,* there I was. If you looked up *phenomenal*, you'd find my name. If you looked up *all that and then some,* yep, there I would be. Yeah, I know, nobody even uses dictionaries anymore, but you get what I'm sayin'.

I am Maya Morgan and I'm off the chain.

I know that sounds arrogant, but it is what it is.

I can't help who I am. And right about now, I'm also the happiest girl on the planet. I was the most famous young talk show host in the country. My television show, *Rumor Central* was still number one (as if there was anything else to be when it came to me). I was six weeks away from graduating high school. I had even managed to pull up my grades, even in that stupid calculus class, which yours truly was now rocking a C in.

And now, I had finally found love with the guy of my dreams. Yeah, I know, at one time I'd thought that was Bryce, my lame ex-boyfriend, but Bryce was a *boy*. My new boo is a *man*. Actually, my new boo is Alvin Martin, my best friend, which is probably why our relationship is going so well.

I dabbed some lip gloss on as I leaned into the mirror and smiled. We were at an Entertainment-industry party, and Alvin had once again held his own, which made me love him that much more. Alvin and I were from two different worlds. Alvin was a geek; I was a goddess. Alvin preferred to stay in the background. I loved my fame. Unlike my other exes, Alvin let me have my shine with no complaint. I couldn't say the same about Bryce, who went to school with me and couldn't stand all of the attention I got, or my other ex, R & B singer J Love, who was always competing with my shine.

Alvin took a backseat and let me do me. Of course, I couldn't forget how well he treated me, nor the fact that he was stupid rich. And now that I'd cleaned him up a little bit, he wasn't half bad looking. I still hadn't been able to get rid of those Coke-bottle glasses, but I was working on it.

I noticed the girl washing her hands in the sink staring at me.

"Hi," I said, when I really wanted to ask her what her problem was.

"Oh, my God," she said, slowly. "Are you Maya Morgan?"

I gave her a small nod and a smile, and she started jumping up and down.

"No way! No freakin' way!" She fumbled to get her phone out of her purse. "Can I take a picture with you?" She was already on the side of me before I could answer, so I just smiled as she snapped a selfie.

"OMG, I'm so putting this on Instagram," she said as she began tapping away on her phone.

"Nice to meet you," I said, dropping my lip gloss back in my purse and stepping around her to go into a stall.

She grabbed my arm and the look on my face must've made her think twice because she dropped my arm and said, "Sorry, I'm just so excited. Just want to say I love your show. I'm so glad they took you off *Miami Divas* and gave you your own show."

I smiled. I was happy about that, too. Although my former co-stars, Evian Javid, Bali Fernandez, Shay Turner, and my BFF, Sheridan Matthews hadn't been too thrilled about it. But whatever.

"Well, I really need to go," I said, pointing at the stall.

"Oh, sorry," the girl said, still excited. "I'll let you go." She giggled as she made her way out the ladies' room.

I hated public restrooms, but all of that Fiji Water (because I didn't do alcohol) I had been drinking was running straight through me. So, I stepped into the stall, thankful that this place at least kept their restrooms clean. I was handling my business when I heard the chatter of two girls as they walked in. I didn't pay them any attention until I heard one of them say my name. That made me stand on alert because of the nasty way it rolled off her tongue.

"Girl, did you see that nerd boy Maya Morgan is with?" one of them said.

"I did. Everybody's talking about it," the other voice replied.

"I'm like, seriously, you dumped J. Love for *that*?"

"For real, what I wouldn't give to have J. Love. He is so fine!"

"Baby, fine ain't even the word. And from what I heard, he was really feeling her and she dumped him for *that*."

Their laughter mixed with water running as I stood deathly still, both angry and shocked.

One of the girls continued. "But did you see him on the dance floor, though? He doesn't have any rhythm."

As mad as I was, they were right about that. Alvin's attempt on the dance floor had been embarrassing to say the least. Still, I couldn't appreciate them talking about my guy like that. Even so, I couldn't bring myself to come out of the stall.

"All I know is I *used* to envy Maya Morgan, but honey, if

that's the best she can do, I think I'll stay me!" Their laughter drifted off as they walked out of the restroom.

I didn't move for a few minutes, then finally pushed open the door and made my way out the stall. I stared at my reflection in the European-tiled mirror. Had I really been reduced to that chick who got talked about in the bathroom?

Were people really talking about my man?

Finally, I took a deep breath and told myself it wasn't about what they wanted. It wasn't about what anyone wanted. I was feeling Alvin and he was feeling me. And that's all that mattered—right?

I shook myself out of my trance, washed my hands, and headed back out. I had just walked back to the VIP area when I saw Alvin standing outside the roped area.

"Hey, babe, what's up?" I asked, wondering why he was out here and not inside the VIP at our private table.

"I came to check on you because you were gone so long and now they won't let me back in."

"What do you mean they won't let you in?" I didn't wait for a reply as I stomped back to the bouncer standing at the door to the VIP room.

"Excuse me. My boyfriend said you won't let him in. He has a VIP bracelet," I said, trying not to get an attitude as I jabbed my finger in Alvin's direction.

The burly bouncer looked at me and then looked at Alvin. "Oh, dude, my bad. I thought you stole that or something." He stepped aside and then giggled to his friend, "I didn't know they were letting bustas in the VIP now."

I rolled my eyes as I stomped past them, Alvin right on my heels. This was the second time tonight someone had disrespected my man and I was getting fed up. I had tried my best not to be *that* chick. But these people were definitely trying to push me.